I0558879

THE MAFIA FUNERAL
and
Other Short Stories

Morgan St. James

MARINA

MARINA PUBLISHING GROUP
Marina Del Rey CA

THE **MAFIA FUNERAL** AND OTHER SHORT STORIES

COPYRIGHT © 2012 BY MORGAN ST. JAMES
All rights reserved.

No part of this book may be reproduced in any form or by electronic or mechanical means including information storage retrieval systems without permission in writing from the publisher, except by a reviewer, who may quote brief passages in a review or brief quotations in critical articles with attribution to the this author. Published by

Marina Publishing Group, P.O. Box 9657, Marina Del Rey CA 90295

Visit our website: www.marina-publishing-group.com

ISBN# 978-0-9837790-3-2

Cover and Interior Design: Elaine McNeal

First Printing

This is a work of fiction and is produced from the author's imagination except where designated as inspired by a true story. People, places and things used in the short stories are used in a fictional manner.

Contact:

marinapublishing@gmail.com

DEDICATION

This book is dedicated to all of the people and organizations who helped my during my journey from novice to novelist.

To my husband and family who always believe in me regardless of what crazy things I try to do.

.

CONTENTS

Sometimes life comes to an end far too soon. When Eliot's friend died at the age of twenty-seven, his wife Susan found herself at a Mafia funeral and wake, mistaken for the daughter of a Mafia Don. Based on a true story.

At age 42, Audrey is taking her first trip to England with her friend Sue. What she imagined as a charming country cottage turns out to be anything but that. However, Audrey and Sue have a completely unexpected type of vacation despite the rocky start. Excerpted from the novel "Confessions of a Cougar," to be released in mid-2012.

Just when Stephen Rollins' future seems bleak, a wealthy old woman named Annie comes into his life and everything turns around. Not satisfied, he becomes greedy.

Love is rediscovered after ten years during a chance meeting. Will they allow themselves to accept it this time? After fate steps in, the decision is no longer theirs. This story inspired Vince DeLuca's character in the novels *Devil's Dance* and *The Devil's Due*

Lillian and Frank have been divorced for more than thirty years. After her fourth husband passes away, she tracks Frank down, and what follows is hilarious... and true.

Miss Molly has lived more years than most. As the sun begins to set on her life, memories of a young love return.

Eighty-year-old Flossie and Sterling Silver are being held by two bumbling Russian thugs. As their daughters race against time to save them, the question is will they get there in time?

Mandy had been terribly wronged, and now she was in an awful bind with no way out...or was she? She discovered retribution is sweet.

Now settle into a comfortable chair,
relax and enjoy these tales.

ACKNOWLEDGMENTS

Writers' groups like Henderson Writers Group, Greater Los Angeles Writers Society and Sisters in Crime. To organizers of the conferences where I attended great additional workshops like the Public Safety Writers Conference, Las Vegas Writers Conference, Left Coast Crime and the many workshops and presentations I attended as I traveled the path. To my family who have always supported my ambitions and my sister Phyllice Bradner who co-authors the Silver Sisters Mysteries.

We learned from each other. To all those who read or have read my columns in Examiner.com and take the time to comment and to the people who attend my workshops and talks—this book is for all of you to enjoy.

Morgan St. James

.

The Mafia Funeral

A TRUE STORY

Twenty-eight-year old Vince DeVarino has died an untimely death. Susan's husband Jerry was one of his best friends and will serve as a pallbearer. Suddenly she finds herself at a Mafia funeral. How does she act when a mobster thinks she's gangster Joey Ventura's daughter?

`

Jerry felt like someone had punched him in the stomach. Speechless at first, he finally managed to say, "What are you saying? That can't be. I just saw him a few days ago—Susan and I ran into him at the Green Walrus. He was with a couple of gorgeous gals. Drinking, laughing, smooching. Why I even teased him about being on a diet. I don't think I've ever seen him that thin, and...oh, shit! Come to think of it, he did have a funny expression on his face when I said that. It wasn't..."

"Yeah, I'm afraid it was. The Big C. He didn't want to tell anyone, you know, didn't want them to worry about him. The family has known for a while that he wasn't going to make it. The Green Walrus. The girls—well, he decided to throw himself a going away party."

"Going away party?" Jerry let a sob escape. "Oh man, that sounds just like Vince, doesn't it? Always ready for fun. But, Angie, he was only twenty-seven. We're not supposed to die when we're young. That's for old people, isn't it?"

"Tell it to the guy upstairs." Angie's voice wavered, and Jerry heard him suck in a few deep breaths before he said, "Anyway, you were his best friend, and I'm asking you to be one of the pallbearers. The funeral is at St. Theresa's this Sunday. I'm also asking Dick, Morrie, Sam, and Bob. Of course, I'll be number six. He loved you guys, and by the way, the others didn't know, either. He really wanted it that way."

Still reeling from the unexpected news, Jerry thought about what it would be like without Vince around. Vince, who said he'd really bucked his old man by opening up a hair salon, of all things, instead of going into what he jokingly called "the family business." He rubbed clenched fists against wet eyes, as he pictured a short guy, probably only about five-foot four, with a little bit of a paunch, smiling chocolate eyes and a mop of jet black hair. Oh, the parties he threw, and the tall women he loved. Vince's latest girlfriend was almost six feet tall and always wore stiletto heels. What was it he said? Jerry rubbed his forehead, trying to remember. Oh yeah. He liked tall girls because his head was right at boob level.

Assaulted by cherished memories of his best friend's magnetic smile and twinkling eyes, he had a hard time imagining him laid out in a casket. Jerry picked up the receiver, then called his wife's cell phone. The words didn't want to come, but he squeezed them past trembling lips anyway, like the last drops in an empty tube. "Angie c-called. Vince—died—last—night. Cancer."

"But, we just saw him. What are you saying, Jerry? Young people don't die." Then she said, "Oh my God. You're serious, aren't you?"

"Yeah, babe. I'm having a real hard time with this."

"Will there be a viewing before the funeral?"

"I don't know. I was so shocked, I forgot to ask. Guess I'll have to call Angie back. I'm still trying to convince myself that this is real, you know. I keep thinking it's another one of Vince's practical jokes."

He called Vince's brother back, and found out there would be a viewing at Graziano's Mortuary. After giving Jerry the details, Angie surprised him by saying, "I did him over."

"You what?"

"Well, when I saw what their idiot cosmetologist did to him—rosy cheeks, fake-looking makeup—I told them that just wouldn't do. So I did him over. That was the least I could do. You know, I wanted my brother looking like himself for his last public appearance."

Angelo DeVarino was one of the top makeup men in Hollywood, and if anyone could get Vince looking like himself, it was Angie. Jerry wondered what it would feel like to apply makeup to one's dead brother. Then, when he saw Vince at the viewing, he knew without question it had been Angie's ultimate expression of love. Vince looked so...so alive.

Jerry also knew that the family business, the one that Angelo had opted not to become part of either, started with the dreaded "M." Sometimes people whispered the word in hushed tones. He always assumed Vince and Angie grew up with hoods breezing in and out of the house, in a lifestyle like the ones in "The Godfather" and "Scarface."

When they became best friends, Vince confided to Jerry that he really hadn't known Angie, Sr. for the first five years of his life, because his father was in jail. That was all Vince ever said about his family, but it was enough. Jerry knew. Still, he had to admit he never expected to be part of a Mafia event, especially a funeral. Just thinking about it made him sweat. Little rivulets trickled down his face and plopped onto his green knit shirt.

Unlike the typical stormy day depicted in books and movies, the Sunday of the funeral dawned bright and sunny, with patches of blue actually peeking through white popcorn clouds, instead of the smog that usually blanketed Los Angeles. As he drove to the church, Jerry even put the top down on his bright yellow convertible, forcing himself to enjoy the beautiful day. His wife's long black hair swirled in the breeze as they traveled the route to downtown Los Angeles, reminiscing about Vince.

Upon arriving at the church, he stared in astonishment at the forty black limousines lining the street in front, even extending around the block, waiting to transport mourners to the cemetery. A man dressed in a somber black suit, black shirt and black tie, shouted, "Jerry, over here," as he sat stopped in traffic. The man approached the car, beckoning to him.

"Uh, you, you're Jerry, right? Pull over here." He crooked his finger toward the curb.

As he said that, one of the limos pulled forward and one backed up, creating a space just big enough for the bright yellow convertible to be fourth in line. Jerry inched the convertible into the spot like a daisy sprouting in a sea of black, then called out to the man, "How did you know it was me?"

After a few grunts that passed as a laugh, the man said, "Yellow convertible driven by a guy with auburn hair? Not that hard to miss, my friend. You're part of the procession." Then the mountain of a man squinted, taking in the whole scenario. "Hmmm. Wish I had a camera to take a picture of this for the guys back in Cleveland. Ya gotta admit, it's gonna be a pretty funny lookin' procession with that yellow rag top of yours and all the black limos."

Off-duty cops leaned against their motorcycles, killing time until they took their positions as the official escorts. Regal palms swayed in the gentle California breeze. Jerry gulped and ran around the car to let Susan out.

As they entered the church, Angie greeted them, then told the priest that Jerry was one of the pallbearers. Inexplicably, the priest narrowed his eyes to glare at them. As Angie walked them to their pew, he explained in hushed tones that the priest was very upset because five of the six pallbearers were Jewish. The priest had insisted the pallbearers should be Catholic. However, he said, he'd made it clear to the old man in no uncertain terms that these five were his brother's best friends and religion had nothing to do with it. When the priest protested again, he'd played hardball. The corners of his mouth drew into a wry smile. "I told him that we'd helped build his church and we could take our support elsewhere."

He patted Jerry on the shoulder. "I added that friends are friends, whatever their religion, and insisted he show respect. The old guy hasn't said two words to me since."

Looking around the church, it quickly became obvious that the limos belonged to several "out of town" mourners. Jerry and his wife recognized some very high-profile mobsters from photos they had seen in newspapers through the years. The five Jewish pallbearers and their spouses huddled on the left side of the church, right next to Angie and his friends. *To genuflect or not?* They whispered among themselves, then finally decided to honor the customs of the church. The priest, now standing at the pulpit, glared laser beams in their direction. Like a scene in a funny movie, the eulogy began.

The priest's deep, resonant voice resounded throughout the church. All eyes remained riveted on the silver-haired Father in his full regalia. As he began to speak with a heavy Italian accent, he continued to stare directly at the five couples. "Today, as we say-a farewell to our son Vincente DeVarino, we know that Jesus-a Christ is-a watching over ninety-nine-a percent of us in this church..."

Hearing a loud gasp from Angie's direction, some of the mourners, including Jerry and Susan, turned to see

7

Angie's face turn as dark as a storm cloud about to burst. Lightning flashed from his eyes. He grasped the front of the pew so hard, his knuckles began to turn white. The priest had defied him. Everyone held their breath, hoping that nothing would happen to ruin the service. Angie slowly relaxed his grip on the pew and his features softened. After that, everything calmed down, the service continued, and finally it was over.

On the way to the car, Jerry whispered, "He looked so natural lying there, somehow I expected him to sit up in the casket and say, 'Okay, folks, the joke's on you. You can go home now.'" Then he grabbed onto Susan's shoulder and sobbed.

The procession of forty black limos and one flashy yellow convertible made its way along the thirty-five mile route from downtown Los Angeles to the cemetery in Tustin, flanked by at least fifteen officers on motorcycles. The heads of drivers in nearby cars whirled to take in the sight, probably wondering which dignitary had died.

At the gravesite, Angie made a point of apologizing for the insensitive comments by the priest and said that he would deal with the situation. Angie, Sr., a short, rotund man with a scar traveling from the corner of his right eye to his chin, wiped tears from his eyes, then took the moment after the final tribute to have his say. He thanked Vince's five friends, and again apologized for the remarks of the priest. His face hardened, causing the scar to look stark white in his swarthy complexion. "In the future, he's not gonna be seeing any more of my dough, and I better not hear of anyone supporting that church no more. From now on, the family will make donations to St. Stephens. *Capice?*" Then he invited everyone to his house in Anaheim for the wake—a celebration his son's short life.

The procession of limos again dominated the freeway from Tustin to Anaheim, until turning off, then entering a *cul de sac.* Angie, Sr.'s house was at the back, with Angie, Jr.'s on one side and assorted cousins' homes around the balance of the circle. Jerry noticed two identical dark green cars parked on either side of the opening to the *cul de sac.* The men inside seemed to be writing in notebooks. "Of course," he thought, "probably the FBI writing down names of anyone they recognized."

Once inside the house, the celebration began with platters overflowing with every type of food, an open bar, Vince's favorite music blasting, mobsters trading stories, a huge mounted photo of Vince smiling down at everyone from an easel at the back of the massive family room, and in the middle of all of it, Jerry and Susan.

He leaned over to her and said, "Honey, I can't believe we're part of this. You know, before we were married, one time Vince said he had to go to Cleveland for a family circle meeting and asked if I wanted to tag along. He said I could have some fun by myself while he was at the event, and then we could kick up our heels on our own. I don't remember why I didn't go. Maybe I couldn't get the time off work." He pointed toward a giant with slicked-back hair, lounging against a bar stool at the other side of the room. "I was just talking to that guy over there. He said he was from Cleveland, and I just happened to mention, you know, about not going on that trip with Vince." He lowered his voice. "From what the guy said, apparently the family in "family circle" was the Cosa Nostra. Vince never said a word about that part of it!"

Susan was about to say something, when a tough looking guy, who appeared to be in his mid-fifties, wearing a broad smile and a beautifully tailored suit, lumbered over to them waggling his finger in her face.

"Hey, baby, ain't you Joey Ventura's daughter?"

She looked around, trying to figure out who he was talking to. He drew closer and tapped his finger on her shoulder. "You. It's you I'm talkin' to. It's me. Uncle Johnnie. Don't tell me you don't recognize me."

"I'm afraid you've mistaken me for someone else. My daddy's name isn't Joey—what did you say?—Ventura? My dad is Mannie Goodman. He's a pediatrician in Manhattan. Sorry."

The man scowled. "Aw, baby, don't be like that. Of course you're Joey's daughter. I'd recognize you anywhere. Those shiny black curls. Why I used to bounce you on my knee when you was a little girl." He snickered. "Mannie Goodman! You coulda come up with something better than that."

They bantered back and forth until Uncle Johnnie conceded that he was, indeed, mistaken. Slapping his head, he said, "Of course," he pointed to Jerry, "this here Yid pallbearer is your husband. Shoulda noticed that." He turned to Jerry. "Bad thing that priest said. You seem like good people. Can we talk?"

Not waiting for an answer, he reached into his pocket and pulled out what appeared to be a whole album of photos. "I wanna show you my family. He pointed out three sons, who appeared to be no more than a year apart and a beautiful blonde couldn't have been more than eighteen or nineteen. After reeling off the boys' names with pride, he tapped the photo of the pretty girl.

"This, here's a wedding picture of my sixth wife, Rena. She's a smart one. Usually I trade 'em in for a younger model when they hit twenty-two or twenty-three. Rena, she knew all about that, so she had the boys right away to make sure I kept her around. Gotta love that kind of moxie."

The guy was likeable in a strange kind of way, but the next day Jerry remembered why he looked familiar. He was Johnnie Mancini. A few years back he'd been accused of masterminding the murder of a few people in San Francisco, but got off, thanks to his slick attorney. The case had made the TV news and the L.A. papers. When the trial was over, the prosecutor penned a book about it, *Getting Away With Murder*. Susan later told Jerry that at the moment he told her who Uncle Johnnie really was, she felt droplets of cold sweat inch down her spine.

They moved away from Uncle Johnnie just about the time a plump woman and her five kids, lined up like stair steps, hustled over. "Hi, I'm Maria DeVarino, Angie, Jr.'s wife. This is Dominick, Theresa, Sal, Maria and the baby, here, is Angie. Figured we'd keep the name going. I've heard a lot about you, Jerry."

"How did you know it was me?"

She laughed and her immense bosom shook like a Jell-O mold. "You gotta be kidding. Do you see any other redheaded men here?"

They chatted for a while before moving on to meet several of the other members of the mob who had flown in to pay their respects. As they sidled over to a handsome man, whose face they recognized but couldn't place, Susan whispered to her husband, "This is wild. First I'm taken for a Mafia daughter and then we learn that Angie has a wife and kids. Who would have thought that?"

Jerry agreed. "I know. He came to every one of Vince's parties with a different beauty on his arm. Truthfully, I've known him for six years, and never knew he was married. Such is life in the *familiga*, I guess."

The party lasted into the night, and as it wound down, Jerry was finally able to reconcile himself to his friend's untimely death. Maybe it was because the wake had been such a joyous occasion. In some ways, he was angry that Vince hadn't said anything. He felt as though he had been robbed of lending his support when his friend needed it most. Then, in a flash of insight, he realized that neither his sympathy nor his support were what Vince had needed.

The party helped drive home the fact that what Vince had needed most was to live his life right up to the last minute, as though it would go on forever. It simply wasn't in his nature to burden his friends or face reality. He wanted them to remember him as they knew him. A happy, fun-loving guy. Thanks to talking to the people who came to honor him, that was okay with Jerry now. Vince just had to live life his way. Sure, he could have chosen to follow in his father's footsteps, living life on the edge, but it wasn't in his nature. It had been easy to see that the hard-boiled members of the crime families couldn't help loving him and honoring him. That love, and respect for one of their own, demanded that they travel many miles to party for him while trying to hold back their tears.

A few weeks later, headlines in the Los Angeles Times proclaimed, "Mobster Joey Ventura shot to death in front of Valley Restaurant in Gangland Massacre." After reading the article, Susan showed the paper to Jerry, and mused, "Guess it's a good thing I wasn't his daughter, after all. One Mafia funeral is enough!"

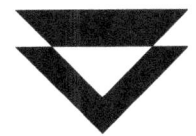

HOW MUCH WORSE CAN IT GET?

EXCERPT FROM "CONFESSIONS OF A COUGAR"

Audrey's boyfriend Bob surprises her with a dream vacation. He makes much of his money trading for everything and anything and just traded for a lease on a cottage in England. He's paying for plane tickets for Audrey and her friend Sue plus expenses, but the charming cottage is anything but that and they are in for more surprises than she can imagine.

As we were leaving the restaurant, Bob leaned close and whispered in my ear, "Don't look right away, but what do you think of that couple over there?"

He flicked his eyes in the direction of a man and woman sitting quite close to each other, heads bent as the young man nibbled her neck. The woman was probably twenty years older than him and judging by the amount of nibbling and groping, it was a good bet they were not mother and son.

Before I could say anything, he added, "Why is it that it doesn't look as dumb when you see an older guy with a young gal."

I truly hate double standards! The only thing missing in what he said was the label we've recently hung on older women involved with younger men. *Cougar.* Sometimes cougars are stereotyped as not-so-attractive old-looking hags with bleached hair and deep pockets— a breed of women who dress cheap, wear hot pink nail polish and favor sleazy animal skin prints.

The woman canoodling in the corner was anything but that. Her clothes were stylish, well cut and clearly expensive. She had sleek blonde hair and what appeared to be a great figure, although she was sitting down. Who knows? Maybe she had a big butt. I figured this sexy woman was in her prime, and imagined her as someone who knew what she wanted and didn't hesitate to go after it.

Yes, a classy, beautiful creature—one who probably had real brains—maybe an attorney or advertising exec. A woman who had attained success on her own.

Without warning, for no particular reason, my daydream morphed into the leopard-print blazer I got on sale at Saks. Cougars might favor animal prints, but that jacket was beautiful. Nothing sleazy about it.

I will admit Bob's snide remark about this woman upset me and I shot back with a little more sarcasm than necessary. "So what do you think? Maybe she snuck up on this poor unsuspecting young guy who's happily nibbling away on his *appetizer* and attacked him."

Bob took another look. "You know, Babe, maybe you're right. She is pretty hot looking and he seems to be enjoying himself. Lots of young guys would probably be ecstatic to have an experienced woman who looked like her give them a tumble. I'll bet she won't even ask if he'll call the next day."

I smiled up at him. "Good for you. You said the right thing. After all, I *am* older than you."

He gave me a hug. Aw, come on—what's six years, Gorgeous?

The following day Sue and I had lunch at the Sunset Bistro. Their food is so scrumptious, gossip has it there's an unspoken rule: when one dines at Sunset Bistro no calorie counting is allowed. They even use real butter and lots of it.

I couldn't wait to tell her Bob offered to treat us to a trip to England. Her smile broadened when I played the trump card. "You haven't heard the best part. He's going to *give* you the plane ticket and he leased a cottage in Surrey. It won't cost you anything but food and entertainment, and you'd pay for the same things here. How cool is that? Come on, it will do you good. Say 'yes,' okay?"

By the look on her face, she already pictured an escape from everything in Los Angeles, even if only for a short time. All the reminders of Hal in their home kept the pain alive. I knew I had her from the moment I mentioned Bob wanted to pay for her ticket. The corners of Sue's sweetheart bow mouth lifted, creating little smile lines at the corners of her eyes. "Your Bob is an amazing guy. Of course I'll go. He's right. I do need a change."

Her pretty deep blue eyes sparkled with excitement. Then a shadow crossed her face, and I knew she was thinking about Hal again. It would take a long time for her to come to grips with his death.

❧

We piled our luggage into a London taxi driven by a man who didn't have a clue how to get to Upper Warlingham, but said with complete confidence he could find it. A bobby in full regalia approached us just as the driver was about to close what he called "the boot".

"Where would ya be goin' ladies? Did I hear you say Upper Warlingham?"

"Why that's right. I didn't realize we were speaking so loud. Do you know it? Could you tell this driver where it is?"

"Did ya fix a price wi' him?"

Sue answered, "No, we didn't since he didn't know where it was."

The Bobby lifted his hand to his mouth, placed two fingers in his mouth and whistled so loud it could have been heard at Buckingham Palace. He signaled another taxi and the driver pulled up beside the one holding our luggage.

He smiled. "This here bloke isn't authorized to go out of London. Simon will take you to Upper Warlingham." He motioned to this new driver. "Why'nt ya transfer their bags and fix a good price for 'em?"

As the man reached into the taxi to switch our luggage, the bobby said, "He's a good man, Simon, and he'll charge you a fair price, not like this bloke." He turned to the first driver. "For shame, tryin' to take advantage of these women. Off with ya now and I best not be seein' ya tryin' this again."

He turned back to us. "Stayin' there are ya? Strange place for two Yanks to be goin' unless you've got business or relatives there."

I felt a little shiver inch up my spine. "Strange? Why do you say that?"

Judging by the tone of his soft, comforting voice, I guess I sounded alarmed. "Nah, not to worry. Just that's it's a wee village. Not even a steakhouse. Gotta go to Whyteleaf for a bite when the pub's not servin', although it's not too far. They do have the one pub in the town square."

During the taxi ride we marveled at the rolling green hills, a shade so rich that it made California look dull. Brilliant yellow fields of mustard brightened the façades of centuries old homes and townhouses. We wanted an adventure and we were about to get one. However, what we got exceeded anything our active imaginations might have conjured.

A little more than an hour later the driver pulled up in front of what should have been the charming cottage we had pictured. Instead, it looked as foreboding as a haunted house nestled in high grass and weeds. The windows were covered in such a heavy layer of dust and dirt they appeared opaque and a few loose shingles made flapping noises when a light breeze lifted them.

Simon's concern was very obvious. "I'm not sure I should be leavin' you ladies here. Are ya sure you'll be alright?"

We had become quite friendly with him during the drive and I could see he felt responsible for us. I truly appreciated his concern, but how bad could it be? We had the keys to the house and there *was* a car in the garage.

Before I could say anything, Sue said, "Don't worry. We'll be just fine." She handed him the pre-arranged fare. He put it in his pocket, but seemed reluctant to leave. "If ya don't mind, I'll just be waitin' to make sure you're alright."

Hey, smart, independent women shouldn't need a guardian angel, so with more confidence than I really felt, I said, "That's so kind, but we'll be just fine. It's okay for you to leave. After all, you have to make a living."

He drove off, and we hefted our cases into the jungle-like growth. To our relief, hidden beneath a portion of the overgrown lawn we discovered there actually *was* a path leading to the front door. Right about then, a machete would have been welcome.

We finally made it to the little porch, but that's when panic spiked our fear. The key didn't fit. We tried sliding it out slightly, pressing it in, jiggling it and every other trick a person can use to make a key work, but it made no difference. Sue said, "What if it's the key to the back door, not the front? Did Bob say anything about that?"

I shrugged in exasperation. Clouds now covered the bit of sun and the temperature dropped. To make matters worse, the light breeze had become stronger and colder. The edges of my ears felt like ice as the breeze turned to wind and ruffled my hair. Smoke curled from nearby chimneys scenting the air. I stood there somewhat forlorn and homesick with my arms wrapped around myself, as if that would warm me. I missed the lovely spring weather we'd left behind in Los Angeles.

"Well, one thing is for sure. We're screwed if we can't get into the house. It won't hurt to try. If that doesn't work, we'll have to figure out which house belongs to the old couple Bob mentioned. They must have a key."

We agreed it didn't make sense to haul our suitcases with us if we couldn't open the back door, so we left them on the porch and plunged into the grass and weeds toward the back of the house. It slid into the lock easily. It turned. The door to the kitchen swung open. My fingers found the light switch and pad for a security alarm on the wall next to the door. I flicked on the overhead light, then keyed in the code Bob had given me.

Sue and I stepped into a bright, modern kitchen complete with red appliances. Okay, red seemed a bit weird, but everyone is entitled to their own taste. I figured the rest of the house would echo the style of the kitchen. Boy, was I wrong!

The living room looked like a set from *Arsenic and Old Lace* modified to double as a 1940s brothel. Unlike the cheerful kitchen, the walls were swathed in deep red flocked wallpaper. A swirl of dusty crystals dripped from an ornate chandelier hanging over two ruby red brocade sofas trimmed with heavy gold fringe along their bottom edges. It was as though unseen souls from centuries past had claimed this room for their own.

"Um, Aud, you met the people who own this house, right? Were they...*old?*"

"Well, I guess Harry might be pushing sixty, but his girlfriend looks like a Las Vegas showgirl. I don't think she's much past twenty-five." The dust tickled my nose and I stifled a sneeze. "I can see why you would ask, though. This place *is* a trip, isn't it?"

In sharp contrast to the dusty chandelier, crisp white lace doilies graced the dark mahogany side tables and lace scarves covered the backs of a pair of forest green velvet chairs. "Well, if nothing else, it does have character," I mused.

"Let's open some windows and get rid of this musty odor." Sue reached behind the green velvet draperies to unlatch a window. Fresh air poured into the living room and she perked up. "Hey Audrey, what do you suppose the bedrooms are like? Race you!"

We sprinted down the hall toward the bedrooms. Not too bad. Fluffy red comforters and pillows perched on high mahogany four poster beds.

"Well, thanks to Bob this is home sweet home—at least for the next few weeks. Let's get settled. Not exactly the charming country cottage I'd imagined, but not bad except for the jungle out front."

Sue shrugged. "I wonder if the whole village is like this."

There was a sharp rap at the front door. I unlocked it and found myself face-to-face with an elderly English couple. The man wore a deep gray V-necked sweater vest, a little gray and beige plaid hat and a broad smile. The woman's shining silver hair, parted in the middle, was pulled into a granny bun. She wore a somewhat shapeless 1930s-style housedress, sprinkled with a tiny pink and lavender flower print, topped by a crocheted rose-colored sweater. For some reason she held a stack of towels and sheets.

"Hello. We're Bert and Mary," the man said in a heavily accented voice. "We sorta look after the place whilst Harry is in the States."

Was it my imagination, or did Bert make a face like he'd swigged spoiled milk when he said "Harry"?

He nodded in the direction of an old-fashioned looking phone on one of the mahogany side tables. "I'm sorry to say, don't be expectin' to use the telephone. There's no service."

Mary leaned forward, as though she was about to tell us a secret, but all she said was, "Y'see, *he* stopped payin' the bill months ago. Just like that bloke, waitin' till the last minute to ring us up about your visit." She shook her head. "It would take a few weeks to get it turned on, but you can use ours if you need to make calls. Besides, there's a phone box in the square."

Bert stooped over and fiddled with a heater. "Here, I'll be lightin' this for you. It doesn't feel a chill now, but wait until tonight and you'll be happy to have the warmth." He toyed with it while Mary elbowed her way into one of the two bedrooms.

She removed two sheets from her pile, laid them on the bed, then went to the other bedroom and repeated the task. "Wouldn't want you to be usin' the same linens as *those* people, you being nice women and all."

The sweet old woman handed me a stack of towels. "When you're ready to go home, don't mind about laundering them. The Tidee-Wash in the square closed about a month ago. I'll take care of cleanin' 'em."

Why was Mary so adamant that we use their sheets and towels, rather than the ones in the cottage? What was with calling Harry and his girlfriend *those* people? I made a mental note to ask.

The elderly couple made their way to the front door.

Mary turned back to us. "Did you exchange money at the airport? Tomorrow's bank holiday and everything will be closed. Bert and I are goin' to Croyden to see our grandchildren, but we'll be back the next day."

Most of the money we changed at Heathrow paid for the taxi. Being Americans, we assumed there would be a bank in Upper Warlingham that offered a better exchange rate. Good luck. On the drive in, we'd noticed this village didn't even have a restaurant or much else in the Square.

Sue's shoulders slumped. "Where can we change money? Harry said there's a car in the garage. We can drive somewhere."

Bert's slapped his forehead. "Blimey, the car! Before he left for the States, Harry asked me to have the mechanic check it. That's what I forgot to tell him when he phoned. The bloke was finally here last Friday and said there's somethin' wrong wi' it—not to drive it 'cause it could be dangerous."

"So we don't have a car? What are we going to do?"

"Not to worry. There's a car hire in the Square. The driver can carry you down to the rental agency in Caterham. You can use our phone to call down to see what's available."

We followed Bert and Mary to their cottage two doors away. In sharp contrast to our accommodations, this one was pristine. From the silver on the sideboard to the crystals hanging from Victorian lampshades, everything sparkled. In contrast to the soft tones in Mary's dress, the colors in their cottage were rich and cheerful. A delicate scent of lavender infused the air. *Why couldn't ours be like this?*

One look at Sue told me her thoughts echoed mine. While Bert dialed the rental agency in Caterham, Sue said, "This is really charming. How old are these homes?"

"Newer than some. Built in the early 1800s I think." His attention turned back to the telephone. "Closin' in three hours are ya? Yes. Two ladies from America need to reserve a car. Righto."

He turned to us. "What's the name? Says he'll stay open for ya and has a nice Morris Mini at a good price. But take care to be there within two hours. He's closin' up for bank holiday and won't be open for two days after that."

I said, "Tell him Audrey Browning, and thank you so much."

At least we wouldn't be stuck without a car or English money, but at the mere thought of maneuvering a right-hand drive car on the wrong side of the road, my heart became a sledge hammer in my chest. We just have to tough some things out in this life, and this was one of them.

A silent message passed between us: How much worse could it get?

RIP OFF

Stephen Rollins was barely making ends meet until he met Annie Forrester, a wealthy old woman who lived in his apartment building. She offered him a way to make extra money and his life went from bleak to comfortable—but human nature kicked in and Stephen got greedy.

Sometimes Stephen's ambition got out of hand, and the end result was never quite the way he envisioned it. This was one of those times.

At first, the idea was only an annoyance. Something that nagged at him while he tried to drift off to sleep at night. Then it began to invade his dreams, and finally it beckoned to him in waking hours while he tried to work. The thing was, it seemed so easy. He strained to remember the first time a little flash of what he now called "The Plan" popped into his mind. Stephen closed his eyes, pulled the lever on his tattered Lazy Boy recliner and let his mind drift.

He had just pulled a handful of bills and dun notices from the mailbox in the lobby of his apartment complex when Annie Forrester rolled up in her wheelchair. The old crone said in a cracking voice, "Hey, sonny, do a good deed and help me get my mail. It's in that box all the way at the top." She made one of those old lady noises in her throat and said, "You'd think after all my complaints, they'd give me a box on the lowest tier. But, no, that young whippersnapper in the management office doesn't pay one bit of attention to me. I'd like to see her in a wheelchair. What would she do then?"

Without a word, he'd taken the key she offered, opened her box and gathered what appeared to be envelopes with checks from various banks and stock brokerage funds. He had a fleeting thought that either the old dame was loaded, or all of the checks were small, but that thought slipped away as soon as he handed her back the envelopes and the key.

Without a word of thanks, she rolled away.

The next day, there she was at the mailbox, almost as though she had been waiting for him. He pasted a smile on his face and said, "Afternoon Ma'am. Can I help you with your mail again?" Truth of the matter was that since his box only held bills and advertisements, it was nice to touch envelopes containing money, even they weren't his.

She gave him an almost flirtatious grin that showed sparkling teeth, and handed him her key. "How kind of you, young man. I kind of hoped you'd be here. What's your name, anyway?"

"Stephen. Stephen Rollins. I live in 501."

"Well, I guess you know from my mail that I'm Annie Forrester. I've lived in this building since it was built. You moved in about four months ago or so, I think. Noticed you and thought you looked like a nice young man."

"Thanks, Miss Forrester."

With a twinkle in her blue eyes, she said, "Stephen, would you be interested in making some extra money? If you are, I think I have something for you."

Stephen thought about what extra money would mean. Depending upon how much it was, it certainly would mean no struggle to make the rent each month, and if there was enough, maybe even a little left over for dinners in a nice restaurant. "What would I have to do, Miss Forrester?"

She patted his hand and said, "If we're gonna be doing business together, just call me Annie."

And that was how it started.

An insistent dinging signaled that the Hefty Man frozen dinner he'd placed in the micro before settling down in the recliner was ready. He didn't have to rely on the cheapest food he could find anymore. Since he'd hooked up with Annie lots of things had changed. Tonight he hadn't felt like sitting in a restaurant by himself and decided Hefty Man would be just fine. Besides, he had a lot to work out in his mind.

After a few more encounters, Annie had suggested that he come to her apartment the following night so she could fill him in on the business opportunity she mentioned. He had a hard time imagining the old woman having anything to offer that could produce much additional income, but he'd gone anyway. When she opened the door, he was blown away. Annie's apartment didn't look anything like his, which was furnished with early Salvation Army. He only had a single, so it hadn't taken much. This apartment had designer furniture, beautiful artwork on the walls and kitchen appliances so modern they looked like an ad in the Sunday Times. The first thing he thought was that the envelopes must have held large checks.

"Sit down, Stephen. Make yourself at home. I made some coffee, but if you'd rather have a drink, help yourself." She pointed to a fully set up bar in one corner of her living room.

"Geeze, Annie, your living room is about twice the size of my whole apartment. Guess I will have a drink instead of the coffee." He crossed the Berber carpet and poured a healthy serving of Chivas Regal scotch for himself. "I'm anxious to hear what you have to offer, Annie. I really could use some extra money."

She flashed what could be described as a perfect Mona Lisa smile. "Oh, don't worry Stephen. There's plenty of money to be made."

With that, she rambled on about some scheme that he really didn't understand at all, but he figured he'd be able to handle it. Something about picking up packages for her from one location and taking them to the Federal Express office. Then going to another Fed Ex office and picking up others from will call. There were a lot of other details, but he had stopped listening. It sounded easy and paid one hundred dollars a week. Four hundred dollars a month, more or less, would make a huge difference in his lifestyle.

"I'm glad you decided to do this, Stephen. I run a little business and it will be a great help to me. By the way, I pay in cash and since I trust you..." She giggled like a schoolgirl and continued, "...and I know where you live, how about if I pay you in advance?"

He almost choked on the words, he was so surprised. "Wow. Fine with me Annie."

She went to a cabinet in the dining room, opened a drawer and pulled out a roll of money that looked big enough to choke a horse. As she stripped off a bill, he couldn't help seeing that it looked like the entire roll was hundreds and there were more rolls shoved back in the drawer. He figured little old Annie Forrester had thousands of dollars just sitting in the unlocked drawer.

"Well, Stephen, here's your money. She had waved it under his nose and handed him some papers and a pen. She tapped a spot at the bottom of the second page. All you have to do is put your signature right here and I'll give you the money. Nothing to worry about, but I don't want people knowing my business. This just says you agree to keep our dealings confidential.

Stephen didn't even look at what he was signing. When he handed it back to her, she smiled and said, "Good boy. There's plenty more where that came from."

That was two months ago. The errands he did for Annie were easy and he definitely enjoyed the extra money, but greed was whispering in his ear. He couldn't stop thinking about that drawer full of money. It would be so easy. After all, what defense could an old woman like her put up? He wondered why he'd never seen her around the building before, but didn't dwell on it. It was more important to figure out how he was going to steal the money. Once he had it, he would move away and Annie would never find him. Simple. He could replace his regular job anywhere. It was nothing special. Besides, depending upon how much money there was in the apartment, he might not even have to worry about a job. One time she had gone into her bedroom and come back with the hundred. The old dame probably had stashes all over the apartment.

He put the recliner back in the upright position and got his dinner out of the microwave. While he forked semi-tasteless Chicken Divan and shriveled vegetables into his mouth, he knew what he had to do. The next time Annie called him up to the apartment for his weekly pay, he would hit her on the head with something heavy and knock her out. He wouldn't even have to bring anything with him because there were plenty of little statues around her apartment that would do the trick. Once she was out, all he had to do was search the place, take everything he found and clear out.

Stephen could hardly wait for the next two days to pass. He hadn't seen Annie at the mailbox and she hadn't asked him to do any errands. He only hoped that nothing had happened to her. That would be a fine mess, wouldn't it? All of his plotting and planning and maybe the old girl had kicked off or something.

"Just don't think that way," he told himself. "Pretty soon you're going to be rolling in dough. Annie will be mad as hell when she comes to, but heck, she made all of it once, and she'll know how to make it again." Stephen was upset that he'd actually been talking out loud, but that's what worry will do. It was too close to have it all slip away.

His normal payday was Thursday. So on Thursday evening he took the elevator to the top floor. If Stephen had been a little more sophisticated, he would have realized that Annie lived in the penthouse. The only reason Stephen had been able to afford an apartment in a building this nice was that after seeing lots of rat holes for the same money, he had spotted an ad for a sublet.

"Lovely unfurnished single, sublet available for two years, single males only apply." A real estate agent had handled the transaction and his rent was paid to the real estate office. Stephen regarded that as an indication that his luck was changing. So, when he'd met Annie, he figured it was all part of his new karma.

As he got off the elevator, he noticed that the door to Annie's apartment was slightly ajar. First he knocked on it with no answer. Then he called out, "Annie, are you in there?" No answer. Had his worst nightmare come true? Had something happened to Annie right on the brink of his becoming rich? Well, unless someone had beaten him to the punch, even if Annie was sick or, heaven forbid, dead, the money was probably still in the apartment. He would just help himself and clear out.

He pushed the door open and stepped into the foyer. That was the last thing that Stephen Rollins ever did. He never felt the expertly placed kitchen knife plunge into his back before he pitched forward onto the floor of the foyer. As his life spilled out on the tile, a woman stepped from behind the door. She shook her head and said out loud, "Funny how it always takes them exactly the same amount of time to go for the money. Man, I hate to move again."

Then she walked to the phone and said in Annie Forrester's quavery voice, "I want to report a murder. The young man who helps me has been stabbed to death right here in my apartment." Before the police arrived, Madeline Stringer, the actress who had been posing as Annie for the past few months, went into the bedroom, took out her makeup kit, and with an expert hand aged forty years in the span of fifteen minutes. She pulled on a silver wig and took the wheelchair out of the closet, ready to greet the police when they arrived. Madeline had tried to make it as an actress for several years without much success. Then, when she got the part of an old lady in a diabolical play, she hit upon what would become her life work and make her a very rich lady.

This was the fifth time in as many years that Madeline pulled off her ingenious scheme.

She would move into a building as an old, disabled but wealthy woman, taking a luxurious apartment. Then she would take another one bedroom or single in the same building under another name. Once things were settled, the ad for a sublet at a ridiculously low price ran in the local paper. She outlined very specific guidelines to the real estate agents she hired to handle the lease. The successful applicant must be a single man or woman, young so that they wouldn't be very worldly, marginal credit report so they would need extra money, and no local relatives. When they found the right person, the apartment was sublet and the game began.

If the person didn't take the "job" she offered, or they were too smart, she bought them out of the sublease, but that had only happened once with a very smart young lady in Baltimore. She had questioned the paper that was to be signed to get the first hundred. While it appeared to be a confidentiality agreement, she immediately saw that the second page, the one with the signature line, was actually an application for a large life insurance policy, available without a physical to people under twenty-five. In the case of Stephen Rollins, the beneficiary was listed as Tricia Applegate, another of Madeline's characters. She always pulled it off in a different city under different aliases.

By the time the police arrived, Madeline had been transformed into Annie Forrester. She sat in the wheelchair wringing her hands, giving the police whatever information she could. She kept fanning her face and looking like she was ready to pass out, so they didn't press her much.

The detective said, "This must be just awful for you Miss Forrester. Do you need me to call someone to stay with you?"

In her best old woman voice she said, "No officer. Let me give you whatever information I can now. I think that I'd like to get away for a while if there's no problem with my leaving. Knowing poor Stephen was killed right in my foyer is making me ill. After all, it's not like I'm a suspect or anything, is it?" She looked at him wide-eyed through spectacles that held nothing but plain glass.

The officer patted her shoulder and said, "Of course not, Miss Forrester. Just leave a number where we can reach you and we'll contact you if we need to. I understand your need to get away. Will you be with friends?"

She allowed a tear to escape as she said, "I don't know. I thought I would just stay at a hotel here in the city until I decide where to go. I can't stay here, where Stephen was murdered, just yet."

The officer nodded. "I understand."

"He was such a nice young man. Who would do something like this? A monster. They would have to be a monster to kill poor Stephen." She collapsed into tears.

Wiping furiously at her eyes she said, "I want to tell you everything I possibly can now and I hope I never have to talk about it again. After all, I don't have that many years left now, do I?"

Madeline made sure she didn't leave out anything. She offered the detective a nice cup of tea. He declined. She talked for at least half an hour, giving every detail she could think of. Then she signed the statement and he left.

That night she left the apartment in the wheelchair, still disguised as Annie in case anyone was watching, carrying a large tote bag. She had scooped all of the money into a small suitcase balanced on her lap. She hailed a cab and went to the Marriott hotel downtown, checked in, and once in the room, cleaned her face and took off the silver wig.

The next afternoon, she wore the high leather boots, tight jeans and tee shirt she had shoved in the tote, applied expert makeup and some brown contact lenses. As a final touch she pulled on a long dark brown wig with bangs and went down to the lobby. Annie Forrester had just disappeared from a room in the Marriott hotel, leaving the police to wonder if it was connected to the unfortunate death of Stephen Rollins.

Using identification that proclaimed her to be Tricia Applegate from Atlanta, Georgia she checked into the Sheraton. The next morning, after a nice breakfast from room service, she called the insurance company and asked for the claims department.

When the adjuster answered, she said in a syrupy Southern accent, "I understand you are handling the policy for my dear friend Stephen Rollins." She made herself sound like she was trying not to cry. "Dear Stevie. I still can't believe he's gone. The last time I talked to him he said he'd taken out an insurance policy and named me beneficiary. I said that was stupid, and we joked about it. I said, "Sure like you're going to die young." He insisted I take down all of the information and said, "You never know. I could be hit by a bus tomorrow, and if anything happens to me, I want to make sure you're taken care of. We were like brother and sister, you know. Who would have ever suspected that would be the last time I spoke to him." She sniffed loudly. "Could you tell me what I do to file my claim? I've never had to do anything like this."

The adjusters' answers were always predictable in the same way she always knew when she had a good prospect on the hook as the tenant. Too bad she hadn't thought about doing this years ago. With millions of dollars in stocks and CDs now, she was able to live nicely off the dividends, but with another $250,000 or $300,000, she could keep a liquid account for traveling and little indulgences. After collecting on Stephen's policy, just one more time and that would be it. She could live the life she'd always dreamed about.

Madeline spread a map of the United States on the bed, closed her eyes and took a stab at it. When she opened her eyes, her finger was on Santa Fe, New Mexico. Ummm. Southwest this time. That would be fun.

She curled up on the sofa and ran names through her mind, trying to picture what the next old lady would look like. Maybe Maude. No, too stuffy sounding. After conjuring up a few more she hit on Arabella. Arabella Unger, retired jewelry designer––her last "paying" performance.

The image in her mind's eye certainly didn't look like Annie Forrester. No sense taking chances. Arabella would be an over-the-hill hippie with wild flaming red hair, dripping in turquoise jewelry. Maybe she would use a silver handled cane this time, one inlaid with turquoise and carnelian.

Now all that was left was to figure out the character she would play for the grieving beneficiary.

Time to book a ticket to Santa Fe.

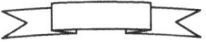

THAT'S WHAT FRIENDS ARE FOR

INSPIRED BY A TRUE STORY

He was her friend and ten years later, when a chance meeting brought them together again, he became her lover. The attraction had always existed but at last they allowed themselves to say the word "love."Then fate intervened.

I was so tunnel-visioned into searching for my luggage, I almost didn't hear the voice behind me say, "I don't believe it! What are you doing here?" At that moment nothing existed in my universe but the fervent prayer that my nondescript black bag with the fluorescent orange tag would come sliding down the chute. I'd already spotted many bags just like mine, but none with the unmistakable tag. It finally appeared just as the voice insisted, "Turn around already, St. James!"

Unless there were a slew of women named St. James at my carousel searching for their for luggage, the remark had to be meant for me. As the bag sailed past, I turned and found myself looking directly into a pair of smiling eyes. A familiar face from the past. What had it been? Ten years?

My hair stylist's partner and I became friends years before, all because of a set of faulty brakes. Like a typical woman, I never paid attention to things like the sound of metal on metal. When I screeched to a halt in front of their shop one day, the whine of the brakes was so loud he rushed out of the shop and glared at me.

"For god's sake, unless you want to be pushing up the daisies, don't drive that death trap until you fix your brakes!" Then in a much more gentle tone he said, "Listen, I'm taking a night class in automotive repair over at the Pierce College. If you bring your car by tomorrow night, I'll fix them for you. I can even get you a huge discount on the parts. Deal?"

I smiled, thinking back to that unlikely start of a friendship. He fixed my brakes, and I treated him to a drink after his class as a thank you. Although I'd gone to his shop for a year, I'd never really said more than two words to him during that time. I won't deny I felt a strong attraction to him, and I guess he had feelings for me too, but before you get the wrong idea, we did keep it to an innocent friendship. It definitely wasn't an affair. Just two people who enjoyed each other's company hanging out now and then.

Two years later I got divorced and moved from the San Fernando Valley to Beverly Hills. As long distance connections do sometimes, ours slowly ebbed away.

Memories flashed through my mind. Visions of us fighting with the Planning Department to push through zoning on a beauty supply store he was opening, trudging around the Los Angeles Arboretum while he studied plants for a horticulture class, driving down to the pier, where he taught me to fish, taking a public speaking class together at Pierce College...so long ago and so many changes in our lives.

I think I managed to keep my face calm, but my heart was pounding. Except for a shadow of sadness that he couldn't hide, time hadn't affected his sex appeal.

He said, "I'm here for my father's funeral. I, um, don't live in California now. I moved to Seattle about seven years ago." He continued with a quick update of his life from the time we'd last seen each other. In the process, he managed to slip in the fact that he and his wife had separated. Then he brightened and said, "Hey, do you have a ride home? My brother's picking me up. We can drop you off."

I thought about my current boyfriend, who was probably already waiting outside for me—a controlling man who tried to monitor my every move. Reluctantly I said, "Sorry, thanks but someone is picking me up. Hey, great seeing you again."

He pressed a business card into my hand, his eyes locking with mine. "Listen, after my wife and I split up a few years ago, I opened a trattoria on Capitol Hill in Seattle. If you're ever in town, call me. I'll treat you to one of the best Italian dinners you've ever had."

Were the fates trying to tell me something? For the past few years, I'd been traveling around the western states working with the interior design of fast food restaurants, and often had appointments in the Seattle area. In fact I was just returning from Oregon. I could feel a grin lifting the corners of my mouth. "Guess what? Invitation accepted. I'm scheduled to be in Seattle next week. I'll call you to get directions." A look of pure joy lit his face.

"In that case, little baby, I'll be counting the hours until you get there. I still can't believe it's you."

"Me neither. I mean what are the odds of us running into each other this way? How did you recognize me?" I patted my mane of auburn hair and he nodded.

"Okay, of course I noticed you changed the color. Big deal. It would take a lot more than that for you to get past me. I used to make my living with hair, remember? If you really want to know what caught my eye, I never forget a great ass." With that, he gave me a pat on the rear followed by a little salute. "See ya next week."

From the time I took him up on the dinner invitation, whenever I was in Seattle, which was about once a month, we spent as much time together as possible. I knew the friendship was turning into love, and he made no attempt to hide his growing feelings for me. When I'd show up at the restaurant, his partner usually greeted me with, "I knew you'd be coming to town soon. This guy has been singing and smiling for a whole week now."

As we shared our experiences of the past ten years, I learned he had moved to Seattle after a bout with cancer, but had been cancer-free since then. Over the next few months, I tried again and again to convince my former boyfriend, who I now secretly thought of as Mr. Control, that he'd been given his walking papers. Every time I thought he understood, he'd turn up with a new way to try to hang on to me, refusing to take 'no' for an answer. He was like a wad of gum stuck to the bottom of your shoe.

During my trips to Seattle, I no longer returned to L.A. on Friday night as I would have in the past. Instead, I took to booking my appointments so I would have to stay there with Peter over the weekends. When I got back home, I'd find notes from Mr. Control tacked to my door. Finally I had no choice but to stand my ground with this overbearing ex-boyfriend by threatening to get a restraining order if he didn't leave me alone. That he understood!

As the relationship blossomed with Peter, neither of us could figure out how we had let this precious friendship slip away so many years before. The more we talked openly about our true feelings, the more we realized the attraction had been there all along. Neither of us had permitted ourselves to acknowledge it, probably because we knew what it would lead to. Although our marriages had not been the stuff romance books and movies are made of, we really did try to be true to our spouses. Now nothing stood in our way.

I found myself pursuing projects in Seattle so I'd have a reason to spend more and more time there. When we were together, I was the happiest person in the world. We did light-hearted things like flying kites and exploring some of the little "Father Knows Best" towns nestled between Washington and Oregon. We took drives to Vancouver and wandered around in the Gaslight area, visited Le Connor, Washington during the tulip season and held hands in public. At long last we allowed ourselves to say, "I love you."

Then it all came crashing down. The day he told me he spotted a knot on his wrist and figured with his history he had to have it checked, an icy hand clutched at my heart. Deep down, I knew the cancer was back. We tried to be positive while we waited for the results of his tests, but they only confirmed what I already knew.

He decided to volunteer himself for an experimental program of intense radiation at the VA Hospital—so intense he had to be kept in isolation. They even collected the hairs when he shaved, and absolutely no visitors were allowed. I forced myself through the days, hoping the radiation would work. He'd kept up a brave front before he checked into the hospital, but I knew how scared he was.

On our last day together before the treatments began, he held me and said, "Look, don't worry. I don't intend to kick the bucket, but just in case I do, I thought this way I could do something others will benefit from. It's going to work, though. It has to."

He spent almost a month undergoing treatments, and the huge amounts of radiation resulted in several side effects, including excruciating headaches. When he was finally out of isolation, he was so sick of the food, he wandered down to the hospital kitchen one day and begged the kitchen staff to allow him to cook a decent Italian meal for himself and his new found hospital buddies. Later he told me he railed at them, "How do you expect us to get better when you feed us nothing but shit?" Of course, they sent him right back to his room, but it was a sign he was getting better. Then, the day of his release finally arrived.

We talked endlessly about what we would do when we knew he was one-hundred percent cancer-free again. He wanted to take me to Italy to celebrate and hinted that maybe we could get married while wc were there. Never for a moment did we allow ourselves to believe he wouldn't beat it. Still, in the back of our minds, both of us were afraid to make any concrete plans yet. But, that didn't stop us from dreaming.

The gods must have smiled upon us. He recovered and suddenly full of energy, he and his partners decided to expand the size of the restaurant in a new location. But it was a bad decision, because the pressure of such a large operation became too stressful. In the end, he decided to sell his share to them.

One day he said, "I'm feeling absolutely great. Want to take that trip to Italy and see what happens? You know, I've been thinking maybe when we return I'll even move back to California."

Sometimes things just fall into place. Once he was free of the restaurant, I had a brilliant idea and introduced him to friends who owned several restaurants in Northern California. I knew they were looking for an operating partner for a new one they were planning to open in Sacramento. With a big organization behind them, it would be a chance to do what he loved doing without the pressure of being the "go-to" guy.

After flying to Sacramento to meet with my friends, he stopped in Los Angeles for a few days, bursting with enthusiasm. "Okay, babe, they figure it will take about six months. It's so perfect. We really hit it off and all that's left is to hammer out the details. I love everything they're planning to do. Meanwhile, you'd better arrange for a few weeks off because I'm taking my best gal to Italy."

I didn't think it was possible to be happier than I was at that moment. I loved him so much.

When I drove Peter to the airport for his return to Seattle, I thought he looked a little tired, but forced myself not to worry. After all, I rationalized, he was still getting over the effects of the radiation and between negotiating the sale of his share of the trattoria, then getting ready to join my friends in their new venture, it was enough to make anyone tired.

During the next few weeks, we existed on phone calls, but I couldn't wait to be back in his arms.

I was in the middle of making plans for another trip to Seattle when my boss asked me to attend a restaurant convention in Reno, Nevada, and made it clear he didn't expect me to disappoint him. Before I left I placed a call to Peter at his apartment to let him know I'd be delayed. I got an open ring which was strange because normally the answering machine picked up if he wasn't there. After I checked into my hotel, I tried again with the same result. When it happened again the next day, I began to worry, but didn't know who to call.

That night I checked my own answering machine. The first message was from my friend in Sacramento. She sounded choked when she said, "Call me right away when you get this."

I dialed immediately, afraid that something had happened to her husband or one of her kids. At the sound of my voice, she began to cry. Between sobs she managed to say, "H-how are you doing?"

How was I doing? What did she mean? Her next words hit me like a punch to the gut. "We were so shocked. Johnny called to ask Peter if he would consider coming to Sacramento a month earlier than we discussed, and...oh, sorry, give me a minute."

She was sobbing again. "Calm down. Did something happen? Why are you crying?"

There was a gasp from the other end, followed by, "Oh my God. You don't know, do you?"

"Know what?"

"Oh my God, oh my God."

The next voice I heard was her husband Johnny's. "It's about Peter, honey. H-he died yesterday. When we called to ask about his schedule, the phone was answered by a strange voice. It turned out to be one of the paramedics. The fellow said Peter had a massive stroke. Apparently he managed to dial 911, but by the time they got there he was gone. I gave them your number. Didn't they call you?"

I sunk onto the bed gasping for breath. "I'm up in Reno. Yours was the first message on my machine. I called you right away. I-I haven't heard the rest of my messages yet." Then like a sleepwalker I got up and paced the room clutching the phone while I cried. I finally managed to say, "Look, thanks. I can't talk right now. I'll call you later." Placing the receiver back on the hook, I let the tears flow.

Mom always taught me to soldier on no matter what happened, and that's what I forced myself to do. First I sat at the table by the window, took some hotel stationery and wrote a goodbye note to Peter, read it, then crumbled it into an ashtray and burned it. I'm not sure what I was thinking at that moment. Maybe I hoped the smoke could somehow reach him carrying the message with all the things I'd never truly been able to verbalize. As it burned, I asked myself why we don't say everything we feel while we still can. Then I fixed my tear-streaked face, pasted on a smile and went down to greet my clients in the Hilton showroom.

Thank goodness it was dark. Gladys Knight was the headliner that night. When she sang *That's What Friends Are For* I hoped my clients couldn't see the silent tears streaming down my face. Trying hard not to make gulping sounds, I felt like she had reached in and squeezed my broken heart with her words.

After the show was over, I made a lame excuse for not hanging around, went up to my room and wallowed in the full force of my sorrow. I fell asleep fully clothed. When the morning sun streamed in through the open drapes and woke me, at first I thought maybe it had all been a dream. But, of course, it wasn't.

It may sound strange, but looking at the ashes, all that was left of my letter to Peter, my spirits lifted. I came to realize how blessed we were to have rediscovered each other, even if it was only for those two short years. I'd been right at the brink of having what I'd always dreamed about with someone I loved deeply.

Time passed and my life moved on. I eventually married a wonderful man, but I've never forgotten how much that interrupted love meant to me. I know Peter's boyish positive outlook and appreciation of life influenced the person I am today in so many ways. Occasionally he still pops into my mind unbidden, and I see his twinkling eyes and infectious smile. That always makes me feel right with the world.

After discovering my love of writing, interior design was left behind. Writing novels, short stories and magazine articles filled my days, but I was never able to commit this particular story to paper. I finally summoned the courage to memorialize Peter as a character named Vince DeLuca in my set of romantic/suspense books, *Devil's Dance* and *The Devil's Due*. The character is fictional, but his personality belongs to Peter...a person who was always a spot of sunshine on a rainy day.

As I wrote about running through a field flying a kite for the first time with him cheering me on, it was as though it was happening all over again. I could actually feel the way my feet flew over the damp grass at Sepulveda Basin Park in Van Nuys, California and my awe at how high the kite was before I reeled it in. In some ways, this story and those two books are my final farewell gift to him—the goodbye we never had a chance to say.

AUTHORS NOTE:

This was a very hard story for me to write because most of it is true. Although some parts are fiction, many of the things really did happen, others should have. I will never forget the pain that squeezed my heart when I found out he had died. Writing as Arliss Adams I was able to use my memories and some of the things we shared to create the fictional character of Vince DeLuca in the Twist of Fate series books *Devil's Dance* and *The Devil's Due.*

This story is a tribute to the real man.

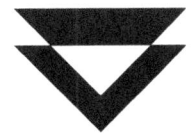

THE SECOND TIME AROUND

A True Story

Lillian's fourth husband has died and she is on the verge of reuniting with her son's father, the man she divorced more than thirty years before. There's only one problem—Her son thinks his father is dead!

Lillian sat in the dark room, her feet up and eyes nearly closed, reflecting upon the loneliness that filled every day now. She told herself lonely people do strange things...a feeble attempt to justify giving in to her overwhelming yearning to find Frank. How could thirty-four years have passed so quickly?

The crazy idea first surfaced, when the sun was still high in a hazy California sky. As deepening shadows invaded the dimly lit room, she remained nestled in the easy chair that long ago formed itself to her ample body. How many times had she picked up the telephone in the past few months, started to dial and then slammed it back in the cradle?

After husband number four dropped dead at the racetrack with a winning ticket in his hand, it just hadn't been the same. Nothing was fun or exciting anymore. "For goodness sake," she admonished herself, "What's the harm? It's time to get a life again." Frank's image began to invade her restless dreams a few weeks ago, almost as though he was challenging her to find him.

Lillian's eyes flew open. "Why didn't I fight to stay with him?" she asked the empty room. She remembered being dreadfully ill after having her son, but what a foolish thing to believe she and the baby were only moving to back home until she felt better. How did she ever allow her authoritarian mother to break up their youthful marriage?

Hovering over Lillian and her grandson, the matriarch fiercely spread her protective wings, making sure Frank never saw them again. Her mother declared that as far as she was concerned, her proper Jewish daughter's yearlong marriage to the tango dancer never existed.

In her heart Lillian always knew Frank loved her and the baby dearly, so the real mystery was how her mother was able to do it. Maybe she uncovered some piece of information to use against him. Why else would he just disappear? Before she knew what happened, the end of their marriage was orchestrated and she never saw Frank again.

What she didn't discern was that her mother really did force him to vow he would stay away, knowing Lillian would assume he abandoned them. As time went on, the hate and disappointment bubbled beneath the surface until one day she just stopped caring and got on with her life.

There was no way she could know Frank used to conceal himself in the protection of one of the doorways across from her mother's house, waiting to catch even a small glimpse of the wife and son he loved so fiercely. Stripped of all hope, after a year he finally gave up and joined the Merchant Marine.

At thirteen, their son discovered Lillian's second husband adopted him, and she told him his real father died when he was a baby. Only in the quiet of her room could she admit to herself that she still loved the dashing Venezuelan tango dancer of her youth. When her second husband died, she married twice more, but never found the love she shared with Frank.

Now, after more than thirty years, Lillian lifted the receiver a final time. Summoning the courage, she dialed the number for New York information. Words tumbling through her mind, taunted her: *Thirty-four years! If you find him, what will he think? Fool! Give it up...*

She would find him! The operator had no trouble locating a listing. He still lived in their old neighborhood. Deciding it must be a sign from above, she dialed the number before she could change her mind.

The phone rang twice. The heavily accented voice of her memory asked, "Who is this?" Instead of saying, "It's Lillian", in a typically coquettish personality she countered, "Is this the same Frank who was once married to a vivacious redhead named Lillian?" (with special emphasis on "vivacious").

Clearly confused, he asked, "Yes... Who is this?"

She pressed on. "And, is this the same Frank who had a son named Eliot?"

There was a catch in his voice as he said, "Yes... Stop torturing me! Who is this?"

She said softly, "Frank...it's Lillian." In the excitement of actually hearing her voice after all this time, his hand hit the receiver inadvertently disconnecting them.

In her darkened San Fernando Valley apartment, Lillian stared at the dead phone. In New York, Frank was completely devastated. To finally hear from the woman he had never stopped loving and then accidentally break the connection with a clumsy swipe of his hand was more than he could bear. He had no idea where the call had come from. How could he ever find her?

Fortunately Lillian's ego didn't allow her to think he'd hung up on purpose, so she called back. He snatched the phone from the hook at the first ring and the sound of his sobs filled the room.

"Lillian...*querida*...I thought I'd lost you again!" There was no question. This was definitely her Frank.

They talked for over two hours. He told Lillian his second wife, the mother of his four children, had died only one year earlier. He confessed that he never stopped loving Lillian and remarried only after losing all hope that they would ever see each other again. He told her how he watched for even a glimpse of her so many years ago. When she asked why he left, he confessed that somehow her mother found out his papers were not in order. The wicked woman had indeed threatened to turn him over to immigration unless he promised never to see or try to contact her again.

As they reminisced, years melted away. During the next month Lillian's telephone rang at the same time every day. The relationship was reaching a point where they talked about getting married again. But, now there was a problem. How would she tell her son that his father was actually alive?

There was something in Lillian's manner as she blasted through the door on a spring afternoon that made Eliot suspect a bomb was about to drop. Without pause she headed for the phone and dialed a number. Eliot never anticipated her next words. "I have something to tell you. Your father is alive."

Without allowing him time to recover from the shock, she shoved the receiver in his hand and said, "Say hello to him."

Eliot had several telephone conversations with the father who had "risen from the dead" after that day, and about a month later Frank called his son. "You must meet me at the airport. I've decided to surprise your mother and see both of you at long last. Don't tell her I'm coming."

They plotted and planned this surprise and finally decided Eliot should invite his mother over for dinner and not say a word about Frank's planned trip. Then Frank could walk in the door and throw his arms around her. But, that was before Eliot's wife pointed out Lillian had gained a good deal of weight during the past thirty-four years, "Please," she pleaded. "She may be your mother, but she's a woman. Trust me. You have to give her the chance to look her best. Don't worry whether she'll look surprised. Knowing your mother, the drama queen, I guarantee you she'll give an "Academy Award" performance. Just let her look good, okay?"

So, late that afternoon Lillian arrived at their home with makeup carefully applied, hair coifed, nails manicured, wearing a very attractive outfit. She glowed with the expectation of seeing her long lost love.

While Eliot was at the airport to meet Frank, Lillian alternated between rehearsing different surprised looks and pacing nervously around her son's living room, anticipating their arrival.

Like a little kid ready to meet his hero, Eliot held up his hand-lettered sign, watching every sixtyish man who came through the arrival gate. He thought it would be easy to spot the dashing tango dancer who swept his mother off her feet back in the day. Tall, probably gray and he would definitely be handsome. As he scanned the arriving passengers, a short, balding slightly overweight man approached him. "Eliot? My son?" The thick Desi Arnaz-type Spanish accent left no doubt that this man was his father. Hardly the Latin lover his mother described, but it didn't matter. He was finally meeting him.

The strangeness of a son meeting a father he had believed to be dead for so many years ebbed away during the drive from the airport. Nearing Eliot's condo complex, fire trucks sped toward them with sirens blaring. He pulled over to the curb across from his front door.

Instead of flying past, the trucks stopped right there. He and Frank watched in awe as licks of brilliant orange flames rose in the air at the back of the complex. Lillian and Eliot's wife stood framed in the open door of his condo, watching the firemen unload hoses and equipment as they prepared to fight the crackling fire. Flashing a mischievous grin Frank turned to his son and said, "*Hijo mio*, Sirens! You sure know how to welcome your father."

Frank dashed across the street and right on cue, Lillian stepped onto the sidewalk, threw up her hands and gave an Oscar-worthy performance. Frank rushed over to embrace her, never suspecting the rehearsals that went into her being so surprised.

They remained wrapped in a fierce embrace, each drinking in the other. Lillian certainly didn't see an aging short, hefty, bald man. She saw a young dark, handsome Latin who danced a mean tango. And Frank didn't see a two hundred and fifty pound woman with flaming auburn hair. He saw the beautiful, vivacious redhead of his dreams. They went inside. She sat on his lap. He winced but grinned through it. She flirted. "There's more of me than you remember, sweetie," she purred in a winsome tone.

"We change," he countered while patting his generous belly. I used to have hair and I didn't have this, *querida*." Gazing deeply into each other's eyes, they were Nelson Eddy and Jeanette MacDonald in a 1920's musical, ready to burst into song. Neither saw the other's flaws. They were clearly in love.

The wedding a week later was a complete scene-stealer. The plan was simple. Accompanied by Eliot, his wife and sister-in-law Carol (who had been a sexy TV actress) they drove to City Hall planning to get the license and be married by the Justice of the Peace.

But the morning's light rain was turning to a violent storm. Traffic snarled in every direction when it moved at all. By the time they finally got the license and asked where to go for the ceremony, the clerk said, "Come back tomorrow. No more ceremonies today." That simply wouldn't work. Frank was leaving in the morning and Lillian was determined they would be married before he left.

So, the bride and groom and their small, soaking wet wedding party all stood in the lobby of City Hall trying to figure out how to make it happen.

"Listen, I've got it", Carol shouted. "There are Mexican wedding chapels all over downtown L.A. I know where they are. We have the license, all we need is the ceremony. Frank, you can translate if they don't speak English." As they headed into the heart of downtown, the storm was getting worse. Cruising the flooded streets like a hydroplane, they searched for just the right place. A storefront chapel with a neon sign flashing Casa de Novios caught Lillian's eye. She called out gaily, "How about that one. It looks friendly."

The soggy bride and groom and their equally soaked wedding party stepped into the front room of the Casa de Novios, which was like entering an eclectically furnished time warp. A 1950's embossed aqua Naugahyde sofa dominated the space next to the counter, a fringed Victorian lamp, gaudy flocked wallpaper and a huge showcase displaying all sorts of veils and headpieces completed the reception room. Behind it, through an elaborately festooned door, was "the chapel" which was really just a boxy room with some folding chairs.

Frank handled the negotiations in Spanish and finally said, "All set *Mi Corazon*." Everyone followed the minister as he walked toward the back room. Before passing through the doorway, in what appeared to be a carefully choreographed pause, the minister stopped, took a slow step backward, turned and said, "But I have forgotten. Perhaps the lady wants a bouquet to match her dress."

With a grand flourish, he threw open a huge concealed showcase overflowing with every manner and color of plastic flower bouquet. When the bride, who was trying not to laugh, didn't opt to buy a bouquet he graciously reached up to a tiny metal cage hanging in the doorway between the two rooms and turned a thumbscrew at the bottom. Instantaneously a mechanical bird began to tweet "Here Comes the Bride" repeatedly.

The minister designated Eliot as best man, his wife matron of honor and Carol was to be the audience. With that settled he got up on a wooden box that served as his platform ready to perform the ceremony. Before he could speak, a very excited Carol rose from her seat and moved toward the platform. "Wait, wait...I can't just be audience! Give me a better part. I can get into character—after all, I'm an actress. You have to give me a chance. If you name it, I'll be it. You simply can't make me audience!"

"Okay", the shocked minister replied shaking his head in disbelief. "Okay, forget the audience...you can be a bridesmaid. Now, can we get on with the wedding?"

The short service was accompanied by the mechanical bird's incessant tweeting. After pronouncing them man and wife, the minister handed the sixty-year-old bride a gift bag of manufacturer's samples to start her married life. Among samples of dishwashing soap and toothpaste was a small sample of birth control pills. She winked and said, "Somehow I don't think I'll need these, but thanks."

Seven years after the wedding, fate intervened again. Lillian and Frank were separated one more time, but this time it was forever. Lillian died with Frank holding her as she struggled to conquer the lymphoma that claimed her body. Like the old song says, for them love was lovelier the second time around!

This story could have easily been the creation of a romance novelist, but I happen to know it's true. You see, at the time I was Eliot's wife.

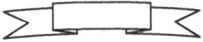

SAYING GOODBYE TO MISS MOLLY

An old lady sits at her window staring at the scenes unfolding in her yard below. Are they reality or simply images from her past paying a visit? To her they are reality, her world as it exists.

There was a time when I wouldn't have been sitting in this chair staring out the window at...what... nothing but a ratty lawn and an old road that goes God knows where. I've been trying to write down the story of my life, such as it is, before I get to the place where I can't remember the good parts anymore. I keep thinkin' someone might care about who I was back then, not who I am now. My memory is just not as good as it used to be.

I put the pen down on top of the paper...can't hardly read my own writing today...and wheel my chair closer to the window so that I can press up against the cool, slightly damp glass. I stare intently, trying to make out the images down in the yard. My hand shakes so badly I have to really concentrate to raise my finger to the surface where I trace my name in bold letters.

M-o-l-l-y. That's my name and I've been stuck with it all my life. Still, it's my window and I can do what I want with it. Besides, I've got to let them know I'm here. The people in my yard.

Molly is an okay name, I guess, but not the one I would have wanted. My whole life I wished Ma had chosen a fancy name like Beatrice or Lillian, or Amanda. But she wasn't that type of woman, not by a long shot. And for some reason I never could bring myself to change it.

Everything she did, everything she said, was plain and practical. I guess that's how she saw me. Plain, practical Molly. A good obedient daughter, able to do lots of chores around our pitiful farm. The whole time I was growing up, I only had one dress each year and I washed it on Saturday so it would be clean for church and the rest of the week. I had one pair of shoes that lasted until my toes scrunched up against the tips and I had my treasure…a beautiful blue hair ribbon that Old Lady Norton gave me when I was six. I saved that ribbon a long time because it was the prettiest thing I ever had.

The other girls wore a different dress every day. I really hated having only one dress to wear to school, day in and day out. One of the women Ma did housework for even asked if she could give her a castoff to take home for me when her daughter was tired of wearing it, but Ma didn't take it. Whenever her daughter got tired of something, the lady kept asking, but Ma never said yes. Not once.

Oh, she would tell me about it and then stand very straight and say, "I told her thank you kindly, but we make do." I cried inside when she said that. "Why? Why didn't you let me have even one nice thing?" But that was her way. Her pride. So I fancied myself in lovely ball gowns and sparkly jewelry. No one knew that in my heart Molly didn't exist anymore. I would be someone different when I grew up. At least that was my dream back then.

My eyesight isn't what it used to be and I really should have some new glasses, but even though I tell them, I don't think anyone listens. One time the doctor who comes now and then to make sure we're alive and kicking said something about glasses not helping cataracts, but I didn't pay any attention. Old people get cataracts. Not me. So when I didn't get those new glasses, I discovered that if I squint really hard for a long time, the shapes start to come into focus. I can just about make out what's in that dark spot in the yard.

One of those shapes is moving right now and seems like it's coming toward the house. Looking through my streaked window I see that it's not just a shape at all. Why it's that silly old dog that used to come by my room and lay its head in my lap. I have to say I miss the old hound. She gave me comfort. It felt good just to touch her soft fur and know that a living thing cared about me. But she doesn't come any more. Getting' too old to climb the stairs, I guess...just like me. I think I'm more than ninety now. At least that's what the young girl who helps take care of me says. But, of course that must be wrong. Ninety is older than any person should be. Things start to go way before that, you know.

Sometimes I get spells where I can see really clear. Those are the good times. Like right now. I can see the dog's huge brown and white head just lyin' there. Dolly, I think her name is. A smile spreads across my parched lips as I make out two little puppies jumping around in the grass as though they have springs on their paws. Where do puppies get all that energy? I'd like to help calm them down. You know, they could give me some of that energy so I didn't get so darned tired just from trying to go down to the social room. I'm much too tired these days. That's why I've been staying in my room a lot lately. I even ask for some of my meals to be brought to me here. One of the puppies jumps on the old dog and she raises her head, stares at it for a minute and lies right back down. I think to myself that's a sensible thing to do. Why let a little whippersnapper ruin her nap?

But the fool little dog doesn't know there's no way he's going to get that old dog to move. So he worries at her and nips at her until he finally gets tired and scampers off with the other one at his heels. Am I getting like the dog, too tired and too lazy to move? I hope not. I wonder how long I've lived here. Years, I think.

I know that I used to own a little nursery school in town. When I got too old and started to forget things, I sold it and used the money to move in here. Assisted living, they call it. I think I was about eighty something, and don't get me wrong. It's not bad. My room is comfortable and I can always look out my window at the yard. There are plenty of people out there. When I owned the school, the children used to call me Miss Molly and I really did love most of them. Now the people who take care of me call me Miss Molly. But, I miss those kids and some days I even miss the pesky ones. Never had any of my own.

When I first came here, I could walk around on my own and even use the stairs. Now they have to wheel my chair into that rickety elevator. I hate the elevator and worry that it will crash to the ground. Well, that's not really it. Not why I hate the elevator, I mean. I'll tell you a secret. I hate that elevator because it reminds me that I can't do what I did before. I'm stuck in this darned chair. And that's downright aggravating for an active woman like me. Well, I was active before I broke my hip, anyway.

Sometimes when I look out my window, it's like I'm looking at the way things were back then. I don't care what they say. I actually do see them, you know. The people that live in my yard. Why it's almost like watching a moving picture. I tell everyone who will listen to me that I'm just gonna pass through my window and be with them someday, but they tell me I'm a silly old woman and I'm seeing things. The young one who takes care of me...she says, "There's no one out there, Miss Molly. Those are just your memories, Hon." How does she know? They'll see. I'll even bet you I'm gonna be out there with them some day.

For me, everything changed the day I packed my few belongings in a cardboard box back when I was about eighteen and told Ma that I wouldn't live her life anymore. I'd found a job in the city working for people who had two little kids and needed someone responsible to watch them during the day.

It was advertised in a newspaper I found while I was in town buying supplies at the general store. Ma decided that going to town would be my job as soon as I was old enough to get there on my own. At least I'd managed to stay in school till I finished high school. Ma didn't want to let me go, but I promised I'd do all my chores and then some. Well, I guess she saw how much I wanted it, and she finally said okay, but to make up for having to say yes she gave me even more work at home. Because I refused to back down, I learned to read very well, do arithmetic and even studied history and geography. I always figured taking the job in the city was my first step in running away from Molly. Plain Molly was the girl who would never be anything.

The Martins had a living room as big as our whole farm house and they had indoor plumbing too. I used to pull the chain of the toilet just to see the water go down and fill back up again. Amazing. They gave me a room of my own that felt like a palace. I would have paid them to stay there if I could. But, of course, I didn't have any money, so room and board and a few dollars for myself felt like heaven. As far back as I could remember, I always shared a bedroom with Ma and now I had my very own room.

Mrs. Martin, the mother of two boys and a little girl, gave me some of her old dresses and it was like she gave me gold. I tried them on, one after the other, in front of the looking glass in my room. She said if I was working for her, I had to look decent and wearing one dress day after day just wouldn't do.

My mind is rambling a bit. I admit that. Seems to be happening more and more lately. Look...there in the yard...the grass has turned a beautiful green and I see Jimmy and Calvin tossing their baseball back and forth.

Those are Mrs. Martin's two sons, and they are a handful. Sure keep me on my toes. They come to visit in the yard now and then. The glass is nice and cool against my forehead as I keep looking out my window. Calvin just threw the ball too hard and hit Jimmy in the stomach. I call out, "Don't you be doing that to your brother." But I don't think he heard me through the closed window. Jimmy falls to the ground. I better get out there and help. It's my job. I try to get up and then remember that I'm stuck in this darn chair. I can see Mrs. Martin taking Jimmy around and shaking her finger at Calvin. When I look again, they're gone. Guess I'll just sit here a while more.

I must have dozed off and it seems like maybe it got a little darker outside while I was sleeping. For some reason the grass doesn't look real green anymore. Wonder if it's going to rain. I do get real sleepy these days, you know. When I lift my head off my chest, I can see that someone brought me a dish of Jell-O. Never even heard them come in. Is my hearing going, too?

I look at the wiggly red cube and think about how much I like Jell-O. Haven't had much of an appetite for a while, but I love Jell-O. Then I notice that the darn girl put that dish right on my paper where I've been writing things down. Now why did she have to do that? There was plenty of room on the table. I pull my chair closer to the table so I won't make a mess, and push the dish off the paper. Then I reach for the spoon, and take a taste. Mmmm, that's good.

When I'm done eating, I decide to go back to my watching, thinking maybe Calvin and Jimmy will come again, but they don't. I guess they got in trouble with Mrs. Martin for fighting. Hope she isn't mad that I couldn't get down there to split them up. Those boys are at each other all the time.

Thinking about Mrs. Martin makes me think about the day her youngest brother came to visit. Lord oh Lord, was he handsome. Took my breath away. She said, "Molly this is my baby brother Benjamin and he's on his way to join the army. He plans to stay with us for a week."

He didn't look like a baby to me, but I think she just meant he was the youngest. He looked at me with clear blue eyes and I thought I was going to faint. Never felt that way about a boy before. Not in all my eighteen years. Benjamin was nineteen and said he felt the call to serve his country. His thick blond hair kept falling in his eyes, and I wanted to brush it back ever so bad, but that wasn't proper. When he spoke, his voice wasn't like the boys from school. It was deep and rich, almost like listening to someone sing the words.

I guess I fell in love with Benjamin the minute I saw him. I was only the nanny so wishing he would notice me as more than a servant was too much to hope for. That is, until I was taking a walk down by the river after the children were in bed one night, and suddenly there he was...walking right next to me.

My heart was pounding so bad I was afraid he would hear it. But he just smiled and said in the musical voice, "Evening, Molly. It is okay if I walk with you?" He told me all about his life in the big city of Chicago and how he wanted to stop here to visit with his sister before going off to war. I remembered studying about Chicago in high school, and was able to ask him lots of good questions. Each one was answered with a smile and the farther we walked the closer he got to me.

Pretty soon he said, "Hope you don't mind if I take your hand, Molly. I think you are just about the prettiest girl I've seen. I don't know why, but I feel like we've known each other forever." Well, I felt that way too and didn't pull my hand away. Then he said something I remembered always. "Molly is too plain a name for a girl who looks like you. I think I'll call you Miranda. Is that okay?" And he kissed me right on the lips.

A movement in the yard catches my eye and I wheel my chair back closer to the window. I think she's out there so I press my face to the glass again. The young woman who comes sometimes. I can't see as well as I'd like to because like I said, it's darker than it was before, but yes it is her. She is just sitting on an old bench in the middle of the lawn. She hasn't been here in a while so I'm surprised to see her sitting so still on that bench. Most times when I see her it seems like she's full of life, but not today. Today it's like she's a statue or something. Her shoulders are slumped and it looks like her body is shaking. Can't be that she's cold. It's barely even fall. I can tell that because the leaves on the trees are just beginning to turn colors.

I call out to her, but I don't think she hears me. Guess I'll just watch for a while. Don't know why, but Benjamin keeps popping into my head. My dear, sweet Benjamin. We were in love before we knew what hit us. The Martins saw it when we came back that night and I must tell you, they were not happy. Oh they tried to act like it didn't bother them, but I saw it in their eyes. "White trash." That's what they were thinking. It was fine for me to help raise their children and do some of the housework but it wasn't fine for Mrs. Martin's brother to be keeping company with me. Not by a mile. She made some persnickety remark when Benjamin finally told them we loved each other. Something about how he hardly knew me and we had to see how we felt when he came back from the war.

Off he went with the promise that we would be together when he got back. He was young but he knew he wanted me. And I wanted him. He stood his ground with them, too, saying they couldn't stop him from loving me. Well, they didn't. What stopped him was a

German bullet. I guess you could say he kept his promise and came back to me, if you could call his cold stiff body all laid out in a box my Benjamin. I was taking care of the boys in the living room the day a man from the army came to the door to tell Mrs. Martin her brother was what he called "a casualty of war." I remember I let out an awful scream and then ran out to the yard and sat on the cold stone bench right by the fence, crying like I would never stop. All I could think was, "Lord, don't let it be true." But it was. The man said he died a hero trying to save two of the soldiers in his company. They lived, Benjamin died. Come to think of it, that young girl I see out in the yard kind of reminds me of how I must have looked that day.

Suddenly I know. She isn't shaking from the cold. She's crying. Just like I cried. You know, four days was all we had. Just four short days. But those days have been with me my whole life. Never loved another man. Never got married. I can hear his voice calling, "Miranda, Miranda" but I know it's not Benjamin calling to me. I don't believe in ghosts. His musical voice will always be part of a memory of the best four days of my whole life. When they threw that last shovel of dirt on the grave, I think I died a little bit too.

I stayed with the Martins another year or so and then Ma got real sick. Even though it was the last place on earth I wanted to be, I had to move back to the farm to help her. It didn't do any good. She just kept failing. One morning I when I brought her breakfast tray, she was laying there so still, eyes open and staring at the ceiling, and I knew. She had passed to a better place. I took the plate of scrambled eggs back to the kitchen and called the doctor. They took her body away and I knew right then I would sell the farm for the few dollars it might bring. I belonged in town, not on this pitiful piece of earth. That's how I bought Miss Molly's School.

I believe the young woman in my yard has gotten up from the bench. I really have to strain to see her. Maybe some clouds are covering the sun, because it seems to keep getting darker. Looks like she's walking toward the fence. From what I can tell, she's wearing a long white dress. Almost like a wedding dress, I think to myself. I look at the empty dish on the table and think," I could use a little more of that Jell-O." Haven't cared much about food the past few days, but the sweetness sort of peaked my appetite. Maybe I should wheel back over by my bed and press the buzzer on the wall so they'll bring me some more. Just thinking about crossing the room seems like it's too much, so I guess I'll sit here a while longer. Don't know why, but I seem to be extra tired today. The whistling sound of the wind outside my window almost sounds like "Miranda." Foolish old woman, that's what I am. No one calls me Miranda. Must be in my head.

I squint a little harder, trying to bring the images back into focus. Why, look at that. She's standing by the gate now and a handsome young soldier is reaching for the latch. I haven't seen him out in the yard before. He's pretty tall and so handsome in that uniform. The wind is sort of ruffling his hair blowing it down into his eyes. She's reaching out and brushing it back. The gate opens and they come back into the yard together. She leads him over to the bench where she was sitting just a few minutes ago. I think it was only a few minutes, but with the way time is for me now, could have been longer. You see, sometimes I just doze off and don't even know it. Maybe I said that before. Anyway, when I wake up it seems like no time has passed. But it has. Can't stop time from passing, can you?

Oh, look, they're hugging like they haven't been together in a long time. He lifts her in the air and whirls around. Wish I could hear what they're saying. She seems to be crying and laughing at the same time. And he's kissing her and holding her. They are surely in love. Any fool can see it. I think to myself that it's almost like watching a silent movie. I can see their lips moving, but there isn't any sound. Most people grew up with talkies, but back in the day when you didn't have words to tell you what was happening, you could always tell from the way they moved and acted. And these two are moving like they waited a long time to be together.

They both stand up, and hold hands. It brings a smile to my lips. Two young people in love. He lets go of her hand and starts to walk back to the gate but for some reason she isn't following. "Go with him," I shout. "If you love him, go with him and be with him." I don't think she hears me because it looks like she's headed back to the bench. "No," I call out. "Don't do that. Don't sit on that darned bench like you can't do anything. Run after him. Don't let him go through the gate." She turns and looks up at my window, like maybe she heard me. Oh, Lord I hope she did. I hope she feels the love for him that I knew with Benjamin for just those few days. It was enough to last my lifetime.

If I could just get up out of this chair, I'd go out there and tell her not to let her love go. But I can't and I don't even have the strength today to wheel over to the elevator. All I can do is sit here and hope she hears me.

When I look back, it's gotten even darker outside. Almost evening, I guess, but that doesn't seem right. Somewhere through the darkness I can still see the sun. There is a little brightness around the young woman and, Lordy be, she's is starting to walk back toward the gate. She's calling out something that I can't hear, and now she's lifting up her long dress so she can run. The soldier turns around, sees her and he stops. I hear him call in a loud, clear voice "Miranda." She runs faster toward the sound of that musical voice and he opens the gate for her. Then she runs into his arms and they walk down the road together with their arms around each other.

When they brought her dinner that evening Miss Molly was sitting in her chair with her head slumped on her chest. There was a smile on her lifeless face and her pen had fallen on the pad next to the last word she wrote. Benjamin.

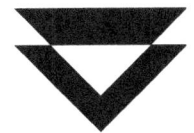

TO CATCH A RUSSIAN THIEF—OR TWO

MORGAN ST. JAMES AND PHYLLICE BRADNER

EXCERPT FROM SILVER SISTERS MYSTERY
"SEVEN DEADLY SAMOVARS"

There is a crime wave in quiet Juneau, Alaska and it all began when Goldie Silver received the wrong shipment of antique Russian tea dispensers from Vladivostok. The Silver twins tracked the bumbling Dumkovsky brothers to L.A., but their eighty-year old mother and uncle, former vaudeville magicians are hot on the trail, too.

Eighty-year-old former vaudeville magicians, Flossie and Sterling Silver, are being held by a pair of crazed Russian thugs. Their daughters Goldie and Godiva are in a race against time to save them.

What should have been a fifteen minute ride to Caesar's house seemed to take forever. While Godiva battled L.A. traffic, Goldie kept dialing Caesar's number, but each time his voice mail answered.

Godiva said, "Goldie, are you sure you're calling the right number? Ricky said Caesar was in the house."

A slight trace of annoyance crept into Goldie's voice as she said, "Of course it's the right number, unless you have the wrong one programmed into your phone. I'm pressing five for speed dial just like you told me to. "

"Okay, Goldie, why don't you try calling Sterling on his cell? Maybe the old dear actually remembered to turn it on. I think he worries about alien sound waves, or something."

Nellie interrupted from the back seat. "Look you two, while you're trying to get them, why don't I call Ricky? You have his number, don't you?"

Nellie dialed as Godiva dictated the number.

Impatiently stomping on the gas pedal, Godiva thought if she speeded up she could make it into the next lane where the cars were zipping along. Just at that moment, a big blue truck filled with tools pulled alongside her and she clipped its bumper with a resounding "whack!" The three women watched in awe as the front bumper of their Town Car flew over the truck and landed on the parkway with a loud clatter. Traffic came to a halt all around them.

"What the...."

Goldie's voice sounded a little shaky. "Umm...Sis, you hit the truck next to us. Guess we better get out and see how bad it is." They stood in the middle of the road and stared at the bumper still teetering back and forth on the grass.

The other driver got out of his truck, looking a bit dazed. Aside from a little dent where their bumpers kissed, he and his truck didn't seem to be any worse for wear. He looked concerned and said, "Are you ladies okay?"

Before anyone could answer, he squinted at Goldie and said, "Hey, wait a minute, I saw your picture on the back of a bus. Don't you write some kind of newspaper column?"

Goldie shook her head and pointed to Godiva who was now walking around the car. "Oh, that's my sister. She's the writer."

Nellie stepped between them. "Look, we have an emergency here. The twins' mother is in great danger and Godiva is really upset. That's probably why she wasn't paying full attention. Can you guys just exchange information so we can get going? Every minute counts."

He smoothed his thinning brown hair over an obvious bald spot and gave them a sympathetic look. "Well, I'm not hurt and there actually isn't much damage to my truck, although..."

Godiva came up beside him, "...although my bumper is over there on the grass and it looks like that's our biggest problem at the moment."

He seemed to consider that and said, "Look, lady, some people would really give you a hard time and lawyer up. You weren't looking, you know. On the other hand, I think my wife reads your column." Then he started walking around her car.

Godiva turned on every ounce of her charm. "Thanks so much for your understanding, Mr..."

"Chet Banger. No comments please. This time you're the banger." He slapped his knee and let out a big guffaw.

While giving him her best smile, she said, "Look Chet, maybe I'll write a special column about the kindness of strangers. I'll put your name in if you want me to."

"Nah. Don't use my name, but you'll have my address. Why not just send me an autographed picture for my wife. Her name is Hannah." He ran his hand along the small dent in his bumper. "Ya know, if you don't want a black mark on your insurance, I have a buddy who can probably fix this for a pretty reasonable price..."

Godiva said, "That would be great. I'm really worried about my mother and I'll include a little extra for you if you can figure out a way for us to get going. Here, I'll write all of the information on the back of my card."

Chet fiddled in his pocket and brought out a slightly crumpled card of his own. He took her pen, scribbled some information on the back, and handed it to her. She read the front out loud, "Banger's the Best... If it's broke, call Chet. Are you a handyman or something?"

"Yep, in fact I'm so handy, I just figured out how to get you ladies back on the road." He walked over to the bumper and picked it up as though it weighed nothing. He pointed to Goldie and Nellie. "If you two will open the back doors, we'll just maneuver it into the back seat somehow and you can drive off." He looked it over and said, "My friend might even be able to bang out the dents and fix it." Then he looked Godiva up and down and added, "But I'm guessing you'll want a new one."

They jockeyed the cumbersome bumper back and forth until it was finally secure in the back seat, with one end of it extending out of the rear side window. Because Nellie was the slimmest and most agile, she volunteered to wiggle in and share the back seat with the bumper.

He called after them, "I'll send ya the bill. Don't forget the picture, and I hope your mother's okay."

Goldie said, "You lucked out, Godiva. Let's get out of here."

They turned a few heads as the Town Car continued along Sunset Boulevard, with its bumper sticking out of the side window. By the time they came to Carolwood Drive and approached Caesar's house, the street was filled with flashing red lights, large men in motorcycle gear, distraught neighbors and detectives from the LAPD.

At first, two of the officers eyeballed them suspiciously and wouldn't let them turn onto the street, saying it was a crime scene and only residents were allowed to pass.

"Omigod," gasped Godiva. "Did anyone get hurt..."

Goldie chimed in, "...or killed? My mother and uncle are in there, you know..."

"...and my boyfriend, too," said Godiva.

At that point, Nellie poked her head around the bumper and called out to one of them, "Officer McPherson, is that you?" He whipped around, surprised to see Captain McNab's wife

She said, "Listen, McPherson, you've got tell me. What happened in there?"

He said, "Well, ma'am, I'm not supposed to say anything, but seeing it's you, Miz McNab, I guess it's okay to assure you that no one's been killed. Outside of a couple bumps and bruises, everyone's fine."

They got out of the car just in time to see the two Russian goons and a smaller stocky man being led out of the house in handcuffs.

Goldie squinted and tugged at Godiva's sleeve. "Omigod, Sis, I can't believe it. Do you know who that shorter one is? That's Rimsky. What's he doing here?"

As the twins and Nellie walked toward the front door, two uniformed officers approached them. The heftier of the pair held up his hand and said, "I'm sorry, ladies, you can't go in." His arm swept the courtyard, which was still filled with assorted bikers and cops. The police cruiser, with Rimsky inside, started to pull out of the circular driveway. "As you can see, this is a crime scene. How did you get past my officers, anyway?"

He was interrupted by his partner, a young man with a shock of sun-bleached hair who didn't look old enough to be a cadet, let alone a uniformed cop. The baby-faced cop said in a surprisingly authoritative tone, "I think it's okay, Mike." He gestured toward Nellie and said a little louder than necessary, "I guess you didn't recognize Captain McNab's wife...."

Goldie put her arm around Godiva and addressed the younger cop. "You know those two old folks inside? They're our mother and uncle. And my sister's boyfriend is Chef Romano. Please, you have to let us go in--we're so worried about all of them."

Just then, Flossie wobbled to the partially open front door with Sterling right behind her. She clutched the doorframe and poked her head out. Godiva noticed she wasn't wearing her glasses.

Steadying herself against the door, Flossie called out, "Oh, it's my dear girls! I'm so happy to see you." She put her hand to her face and felt around where her glasses should have been. "Well, actually, I can't see you very well at all, but I sure can hear you."

Goldie sprinted up the stairs and gave her mother a bear hug. "Oh, Mom, we were so worried about you." Then she noticed that Flossie was sporting a real shiner. She touched her mother's cheek gently. "What have those ruffians done to you? You've got a black eye and a cut on the side of your face."

Flossie touched her brow and winced. She balled her hands into fists and threw a mock one-two punch. "If you think this is bad, you should see the other guy!"

She looped her arms through those of her daughters and tut-tutted, "Black eye, schmack eye. It'll heal up. Just wait'll we tell you what happened." Sterling shook his head as if to say, "Your mother and her crazy ideas."

Waggling her finger at the fuzzy image of her brother-in-law, the twins' mother chattered away. "Your uncle and I were just like a pair of comic book heroes, weren't we Sterling? You see girls, I got this idea for a real doozy of a trick to..."

Sterling harrumphed. "You and your ideas will get us killed some day, Flossie. I don't know how you manage to talk me into them."

Godiva shook her head, looking at the broken glass in the front door. In spite of the ordeal, Flossie was radiating excitement and seemed much younger than her eighty-one years. Even though Sterling leaned heavily on his cane, there was also a spring in his step.

"What am I going to do with you two? You're worse than a pair of wayward teenagers."

Nellie patted Godiva on the arm. "I know what you mean. Harley's folks are a handful too. They're in their mid-eighties and, of all things, they've taken up skydiving. I worry about them every day. But my mother-in-law just says, 'I used to be afraid that sky-diving might kill me, but now that I'm so close, I figure, what a way to go!'"

The group made their way to the living room, carefully stepping around the mess in the long entry hall. Caesar settled Sterling into an easy chair and brought an ice bag for the bump on his head and a cool damp cloth for Flossie's wounds. Then he sat on the sofa next to Flossie and dropped his head into his hands. Two LAPD officers, still in the house, continued to wrap things up.

In a voice filled with fury, Godiva shouted, "Caesar, how could you do this? You knew the house was under surveillance...you knew those thugs were going to come after the samovar and still, you allowed my mother and uncle to be in this dangerous situation." She raised a balled fist in his direction. "Caesar...*no one* but you was supposed to be in the house. You all could have gotten killed."

He raised his head and flashed an apologetic half-smile, holding his hands up in protest. "*Cara mia*, I know you're mad at me, but that isn't quite how it happened. Just let me tell you..."

Sterling broke in. "Listen girls, your mother and I take full responsibility. First we lied to you about going to dinner and a movie. Heck, I have no idea what movies are playing at the Beverly Center tonight, but it sounded good. Then we bullied Caesar into letting us come over because Flossie hatched a clever plot to catch the villains."

"Yeah, and it would have worked, too," said Flossie, "if it wasn't for that other guy. I thought there were only two."

"And what about the motorcycle gang! Where did they come from, anyway?" croaked Sterling, "I almost peed my pants when they revved things up."

Goldie said, "Well Mom, you won't believe it, but I know who the third guy is. He's Rimsky...the fellow who takes care of Father Innocent back in Juneau. Belle said he disappeared a few days ago. When she told me the church ladies couldn't find him, I didn't think anything of it. After all, I hardly know him, and he struck me as a kind of stupid guy. I have no idea how he's involved in all of this or if he even knows the Dumkovskys."

"Don't let him fool you," Sterling snorted. "That guy is one smart cookie and he's after the samovars, too. He got here first, disguised as a Food Broadcasting messenger. When those two other goons broke in, they did seem to know each other. If I remember right, they called him by name." He readjusted the icepack, positioning it around the spot where Rimsky hit him with the gun. Although he made a point of appearing to tough it out, a small groan escaped.

After that, everyone started to talk at the same time. Finally Caesar put two fingers to his lips and let out a shrill whistle. "Stop, stop. This isn't getting us anywhere. Settle down and let me tell all of you what happened."

The twins sank down into the lounge chairs on either side of the fireplace and stared at him stony-faced. Nellie pulled up a side chair. Both officers stopped what they were doing and stood a little closer, arms akimbo, waiting for Caesar to start.

He cleared his throat, and then cleared it again, stalling for time. When he cast a hopeful glance at Godiva, she did not smile back at him. "Well, like your uncle said, the shorter guy got here first. He's a mean one, that... that... what is it, Ritzsky?"

Goldie's voice dripped icicles. "Rimsky."

"Anyway, Sterling told him I didn't have the samovar, but he was still demanding that I give it to him when your Dumkovskys smashed the window. As soon as they came face-to-face, Sterling is right...they recognized each other. Then it got pretty rowdy with all of them shouting at each other in Russian."

Sterling said under his breath, "Cursin' each other, if you ask me."

Flossie reached over and patted Caesar's knee. "You're not telling the whole story. You left out the part where the first guy pretended he had papers from your studio."

"We said he got here first, dressed like a messenger," he answered through clenched teeth.

"Yes, but you didn't say how he got into the house." She smiled triumphantly at her daughters. "Pretty clever saying he needed a signature. While Caesar went to the door, your uncle and I waited in the dining room."

Sterling perked up, "At least we got to sample that wonderful dish you made. You should take a taste, girls."

"It was good wasn't it?" said Caesar, "I used some vegetables, veal...I was thinking of naming it after you, *Cara Mia*."

"...Enough, Caesar! Sure it was good," Flossie interrupted, "but we were about to tell you our scheme to catch the crooks when that *schlemiel* barged in. Instead of dazzling you with how clever we are, we see this guy with a gun shoved in your back pushing you down the hall."

Sterling added, "Anyway, we were doing a pretty good job of hiding until I stepped on your mother's toe, and she shouted that I'm a klutz. Of course, the minute he heard her shrieking, he knew Caesar wasn't alone."

The old woman mouthed, "Sorry."

"But she made up for it when he told her to tie me up. That old girl used the Knot of Deception, you know, the one your Dad invented. Anyway, he didn't suspect a thing and as soon as he left the room, I was able to wiggle out of the rope and untie Flossie. Then we..."

"Sterling...Flossie...there is time for that later." Caesar sounded miffed, as if he felt they were stealing his thunder. "Here's the important part. After the Dumkovskys broke in, and saw the other guy here, one of them starts to strangle him. That was some fight! Two against one, but that Rimsky was not one to tangle with. I tell you, what he lacks in size, he makes up for in nastiness."

Everyone in the room waited for the chef to continue his story. Caesar walked over to the window and started pacing, clearly struggling to remember the events of the evening. Finally he tapped his finger against his chin and said, "All of a sudden one of the Dumkovskys spots a leather bag hanging around that other guy's neck." Caesar grabbed at the air. "He lets out a roar and yanks it off."

"...a leather bag?"

"Yeah, it was a little tiny bag, like one of those Indian medicine bags or something. He spits in Rimsky's face and shouts in English, 'Traitor!' Then he tosses it to the other Dumkovsky who yells something back in Russian. That one takes a little tin out of his pocket, opens it up, and stuffs the bag inside."

Flossie was wiggling around like a kid who needed a bathroom break. Without her glasses, she was squinting so much that her eyes were nearly closed. "Don't forget my part." She turned in the direction of the twins. "I tell you girls, I was just like Wonder Woman, wasn't I, Caesar?"

"I'm getting to that Flossie. Calm down." He stopped pacing and sat down on the sofa again. "The second Dumkovsky is standing there looking at the box in his hand when your mother comes out of the dining room swinging a big brass candlestick and whacks him right in the face."

Flossie clapped her hands and chuckled with delight. "Yep, I ended up ass over teakettle there on the couch. Good thing I had my new Lollypops underwear on!"

"You should have seen your mother. She really gave him a good one. Blood's dripping everywhere; he's holding his nose and cursing in Russian. That's when those motorcycle maniacs busted in whooping and hollering while more of them were out in the courtyard making a god-awful racket with their engines. We thought it was an earthquake. Not far behind them were the cops." He took a deep breath. "You know the rest of the story."

Nellie spoke up from her chair by the fireplace. "I'm just glad everyone is okay. Sounds like the Riders had fun, too. They love a good fight. I'm glad my husband called them."

Goldie said, "Yeah, Nellie. So am I." She looked lovingly at her mother and shook her head. "Mom, I can't believe you did that. You really whacked him?"

She nodded, holding up her right fist like a champ. "To tell you the truth, it's a wonder I hit anything. I lost my glasses when that creep hit me so I just came out swinging. I figured I'd hit someone. I was praying it wouldn't be you, Caesar."

Everyone sank back into their seats looking exhausted. The policemen began to wrap things up. Nellie said, "Well, Flossie and Sterling, you've had quite a night. We should be getting you home, don't you think?"

"What should I do about the broken window in my front door?" Caesar threw his hands in the air, looking helpless. "I'll never get anyone out to fix it this late."

Goldie said, "Calm down, Caesar. Surely you have a hammer and a few nails around here somewhere. Maybe there's a piece of wood in your garage we can nail over the opening."

He shrugged. "I guess I can find something. But who can we get to put it up?"

She patted him on the arm. "No big deal, Caesar. I can do it for you." One of the cops stifled a chuckle and Godiva received the message from her sister loud and clear: *He's useless.*

Caesar stalked off to the garage and came back with a hammer and nails and a piece of wood from an old packing crate. He insisted he could do it himself, but after hitting his thumb twice and bellowing in pain, he surrendered the hammer to Goldie. She finished the job in less than five minutes, put the hammer on the hall table and said, "Okay, let's get going."

My car's got the bumper in the back seat," Godiva said, "so I think I'll leave it here at Caesar's and ask the dealership to pick it up tomorrow. I suppose Sterling's old Caddy can hold all of us."

Sterling's shoulders sagged. He looked down at his feet and sighed, "I'm sorry girls, I'm just too tired to drive it home."

Goldie got up and put her arm around her uncle's shoulder, "No problem, Unk. I drive Red's truck all the time...your Cadillac should be a piece of cake for me. We'll put two of us in the front, and three in the back. What do you say?"

He put down the ice pack and nodded.

Godiva turned to Caesar and said in a flat tone, "I'll call the dealership tomorrow morning to pick up my Town Car. We'll come back over in the roadster to meet them and sign whatever paperwork they need to haul it away."

Caesar reminded Godiva that he had to be at the studio early in the morning to make preparations for his show. He tried to put his arm around her waist, but she threw it off, still angry. "Godiva, I'm sorry. Flossie and Sterling said they had such a good idea, and I never even got to hear it."

She snapped, "And you won't..."

He reached in his pocket and then pressed a house key in her hand. "Here, *Cara Mia*, just use this tomorrow. That way you can wait for the driver inside."

With the Russian thugs safely in custody, the oldsters safe and the secret that made the samovars worth killing for about to be revealed, everything was finally under control—or was it?

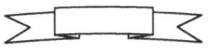

.

WHAT HAPPENED TO MANDY BLAKE?

When Mandy met Mark she was sure he was more than any woman could hope for. So sure, a month later she moved in with him. Love turned to hate and finally fear for her life. But she has vowed to find a way out.

I juggled the bag containing little white cartons of Chinese takeout as I tried to fit my key in the door. Why at times like this did the key seem to belong to someone else's house? I wriggled back and forth, hoping I could make it to the bathroom on time.

As I finally managed to open the door, the shrill sound of a ringing phone greeted me. I grumbled under my breath, "Just what I needed." Bathroom or phone? I exchanged the bag for the receiver on my way to the powder room.

Brittany bombarded me before I could even say hello. "Mandy, drop whatever you're doing. Grant Corrigan invited me to a party tonight."

I managed to say, "Hold on a sec. I just got in and I need to pee." My vision of a quiet evening ebbed away like the tide going out to sea. A few moments later I was able to say, "Okay, I'm back. What's this about a party? Who is Grant Corrigan?"

"Only *The Grant Corrigan*, that's who. You know...the big A-list agent. But then, I guess there's no reason *you* should know his name. He handles a stable of Hollywood's best. My god girl, you can't turn on a TV entertainment news show without hearing something about one of them. Come on Mandy, you have to come with me for moral support. I'll pick you up in an hour. Be ready."

Before I could protest, the staccato dial tone beeped in my ear. No rest for the weary, I guess. I rationalized that friends have to support friends. I knew Brittany would be there in a minute if I needed help. For an up and coming actress like her, this was the equivalent of a winning lottery ticket.

I dragged myself into the bedroom, shuffled through my party dresses and pulled out a sleek "perfect everywhere" little black dress and some very sexy stiletto sandals. By the time Brittany's Mercedes pulled up in front of my townhouse, I'd actually managed to slip into a party mood.

Why didn't I stay home?

I hadn't been there ten minutes when Mark Barton spotted me and introduced himself, then didn't leave my side all night. I have to confess, I was impressed. What woman wouldn't be? Rich, good looking and romantic, Mark was the guy every woman dreams about. I was never one to make snap decisions, so even I was surprised when a month later I leased out my townhouse and moved into his magnificent home right on the sand of Malibu beach, playground of the rich and famous. That was last year.

Noisy gulls chattered overhead as waves crashed on the shore. Did you know when those waves hit it can feel like a small earthquake? Something you get used to, I guess. I hardly heard Mark sneak up behind me. With both hands on my shoulders, he turned me around to face him. A light breeze carried the salty aroma of the sea into the house through open French doors.

Mark has a shock of surfer blond hair that tumbles over his forehead giving him a boyish devil-may-care look. I tilted my head up to look at him and gazed into his ice blue eyes. They were as frigid as glacial ice this morning. A shudder traveled my body because I'd learned to recognize what that look meant. In the beginning I'd been so deceived by this handsome, loving man. For one thing, he is anything but the good-natured fellow he appears to be. He's a cruel, calculating man, capable of almost anything. I'd been so blind.

"Mandy, it's time for you to make another trip for me. Amsterdam. You'll be meeting Ansel again in Amsterdam. Go to the same small gift shop in Dam Square. He'll give you a gift-wrapped box containing a small, gaudy souvenir statue. The body of the windmill is covered with what will appear to be rhinestones. Quite well done, actually. With that many large stones and the tacky paint, no one will ever suspect that they're diamonds and emeralds. Everything will be the same as the other times. When you go through customs, if anyone asks, say it's a present for your mother."

"--Diamonds? Emeralds?"

"Of course, my dear. About three million dollars worth this time. Sprayed down to dull the luster, our little treasures look just like a cheap knick-knacks. There's no way anyone will ever suspect this one is worth a fortune."

"Mark, I'm scared. I can't do it again. One of these days I'm going to get caught."

"Calm down. Why would you think that? You're a clever, respected businesswoman. You make frequent international buying trips," he raised an eyebrow, "and have for several years now. Don't you usually bring back something for your mother? I'll bet the customs folks are so used to seeing you, they probably know you by name, particularly the guys." He snickered, allowing his eyes to travel up and down my body in a lecherous way. "Be honest. How hard does anyone inspect what you bring in anymore? You know just which line to go through."

My hands curled into fists at my side. With my heart beating like a drum solo, I shouted, "I won't go. I won't do it again. You can't make me."

"Ah, but I can," he shouted back, then grabbed me by the hair and forced me to look into his icy glare. "And I will! After all, Mandy, you know I can hang you with what I have."

Hatred for the man I once loved, washed over me. He hissed, " You're so photogenic, my dear. Those videos of you picking up the first package for me, and all the others after that, are priceless. He threw back his head and laughed. It was a cold mirthless sound, not one of joy. "Let's just call them my insurance policy."

He tightened his grip. "You were absolutely perfect on the one with my actor friend showing you how to behave when you went through customs on that first trip." His face lit with delight. "Of course, back then you had no idea you were carrying anything but trinkets, but who would ever believe you now?"

I stared at him without saying a word. He shrugged. "Still, my favorite is the one from your last trip. I really loved showing you that one. You didn't know you starred in a series of videos until then."

Prickles of anxiety accompanied a cold chill. The tapes. Somehow he had recorded every move I'd made beginning with my first trip for him.

His voice rose, "Honey, if you don't do what I want, I'll put you away..."

My God, he can say I planned everything. I took a strong stand, trying not to give in to the panic growing within me. "You know if you use those tapes against me, I won't be the only one in trouble." I paused, suddenly confused. "Wait a minute. You said actor. Who are you talking about? I never met anyone but Ansel."

Mark squeezed my shoulder hard enough to make me cry out. "You're so naïve for a smart person, Mandy. There is no Ansel. He's a person I created. If you don't make the trip, "Ansel" simply vanishes, because he never existed. What happens to your crazy story about me then?"

I tried to protest, but he continued. "Your threats mean nothing. If you swear I'm behind it, all anyone will see on those tapes is you on camera with a shadowy image. Ansel is nothing more than a phantom. Maybe you didn't notice, he never faces the camera. In fact, the only one those tapes will convict is you. It really looks like you're plotting strategies with your accomplice. There is absolutely nothing to put me in the picture."

I knew he was right. My mind raced trying to figure out what to say next.

"So, why don't you be a good little girl and prepare for your trip? If you don't do this for me, you'll be the only one going to prison, and it'll be for a long, long time. Trust me, I will use what I have."

Without thinking before I spoke, I asked, "If you use those tapes against me, how will you explain having them?"

"Oh Mandy, you're so dense. That'll be easy. I'll just say the maid found these lying on the floor in your office when she was cleaning. She didn't know what to do with them and gave them to me. Hey, I'm an honest guy. They weren't labeled, so I watched them and what I saw shocked me. I had to do my civic duty, didn't I?"

I felt like slapping him, but stood frozen to the spot.

"Mandy, Mandy, how could I know you were a smuggler and a crook when I asked you to move in? I'll say at first I figured maybe "Ansel" was blackmailing you with the tapes, but being so honest and all, I couldn't let that be my problem. By the way, if you remember, you did put the tickets and hotel on your own cards every time. I mean, how could I know what you were up to? Lucky you didn't steal from me. See what I mean? Nothing to tie anything to me."

An icy chill slid down my spine as I studied him, knowing that he could do exactly what he said and get away with it. I guess that's all I was to him-- a way to get the job done. I could be replaced in a heartbeat, and he would claim total innocence.

My mind was racing at warp speed. I couldn't slow it down. Perspiration dotted my forehead, little droplets sliding down into my eyes. The words echoed in my head, *"Trapped...trapped ..."*

In the early days of our relationship I really did think he loved me. I was crazy in love when I moved into this house and expected my life to be heaven, but now I'm living in hell.

Back then I did everything he asked without question. However, curiosity about the souvenirs Ansel gave me each time finally got the best of me. I thought maybe it was a quirk of Mark's, so I asked. The answer Ansel gave me that day was hardly what I expected. I was furious and when I got home I confronted Mark. That's when he showed me the first tape.

I could still feel the disbelief that washed over me as I watched that video. He taunted me, a smirk transforming his handsome face. "Mandy, it wasn't an accident that we met. I handpicked you, did you know that? You walked into the party, I spotted you and thought you could be the one. I saw that you were with Brittany, so before I approached you I got a little background. That girl loves to talk.

Then when you told me all about yourself, by the end of the evening I knew I was right. Actually, it surprised me that you agreed to move in so fast, but then you're used to making fast decisions. I guess that's how you built a good business. When you talked about your frequent trips abroad it was the final piece. You were perfect. The woman I'd been looking for."

He walked over to the bar and poured himself a vodka. "Want one?" He offered me the drink as though nothing was wrong.

"It's a definite bonus that you're beautiful and hot in bed. The way I see it, without these," he tapped the pile of tapes on the cabinet, "no one would ever suspect what you're up to."

He played two more tapes to make his point. The first one showed me asking questions about getting through customs. The conversation was set up to make it look like I knew what I was carrying. I swear. I had no idea. The second tape, the one recorded on the last trip, about the time I started to suspect something was off, featured "Ansel" showing me a sample of the quality of diamonds and emeralds I was carrying. We discussed what I should say so candidly that it was the equivalent of a "smoking gun." I looked as guilty as sin on that tape.

I couldn't stop my hands from shaking. A tight band of fear wound around my chest. It hurt to breathe. How could I have been so foolish? I felt like crying, but instead I said, "You know you're really a monster. What if..." I hesitated, my voice dry and raspy. "What if I decide to pay the price? Let the police arrest me. I can't continue to do this-this smuggling. You've made me your captive, You're disgusting!"

An arrogant sneer played around his mouth. He spat out, "Aw, Mandy. Think of the embarrassment. Your name plastered all over the papers. Worse yet, you *will* go to prison. I'll make sure of that. Can't you see it? "Antique Importer Mandy Blake Smuggles Millions--All

Caught On Tape." And, someone like you in prison, oh baby, they will *love* you! Now be a good girl. Knock off this foolishness and just do what I ask you."

I swiped at the tears welling in my eyes. It wasn't supposed to be like this. My friends and family thought I had a storybook life filled with celebrity parties, trips and excitement. How could they know? And me? Well I was drowning in the spiral of a black whirlpool.

He stormed out, throwing over his shoulder, "Book those tickets and behave yourself. Don't wait up for me." I knew he planned to leave the next afternoon for Mexico City and wouldn't be back until late the following night.

As time slipped by, I sat on the deck, sipping a chardonnay, trying to concentrate on some porpoises darting through the waves. *If only life was as simple for me as it is for them.*

After I discovered what Mark tricked me into doing, I thought about telling the police everything and begging to be put in some sort of protection plan, but it would be my word against his. Mark has connections at every level, even violent ones. I sat there looking at the welcoming ebb and fall of the ocean, and just like that the truth hit me in the face.

My rational mind fought the truth, but as the tears ran down my face, I knew. He didn't intend to use the tapes to send me to prison. He was going to have me killed and use the tapes to make it look like I couldn't face exposure and committed suicide.

The only reason he showed me the tapes was to keep me quiet for as long as he needed. The message I'd seen in his face was clear as the letters on a theater marquee. The moment I threatened him, I'd become the walking dead. That did it. My decision was made.

I had to beat him to the punch. Unable to sit still, I stumbled back into the living room with its limestone floors and beautiful raw silk furniture. When I said I might go to the police, I had just signed my own death warrant. I wouldn't let him have me killed and make it look like suicide. I had a plan too. If nothing else, I'd make him pay for what he did to me.

I climbed the circular staircase to my office on the second floor, and had to sit down on a step about half way up as dizziness overwhelmed me. My mother always told me an ounce of prevention was worth a pound of cure. After he showed me the tapes, I wrote two letters that I thought of as my insurance policy. Mom's words echoed in my head as I formed the nucleus of a plan. The way things were going, I had to prepare for the worst. As it turned out, it was a good thing I did.

It was time. With firm resolve, I removed the letters from their hiding place, wrote today's date, added the rest of the contents from the drawer and sealed the envelopes. Then I drove the short distance to the mailbox.

The next morning Mark left around eight. After that I arranged things so they were exactly the way they had to be for my plan to work. Next I dialed Brittany's number. I knew she was working on a movie and had an early call. I made my voice thin and shaky on her voice mail.

"Hey Brit, I've got to get out of here. I'm really in trouble and I can't take it anymore. Mark is-is threatening my life." Long pause. "I'm so afraid. Where are you?" After another pause, obviously fighting off tears, I made my voice rise. "I-I..." and then I threw a statue across the room and it landed on the limestone floor with a loud crack. I banged the receiver down.

Next, I called 911. "I need help. I..." Stopping in mid sentence, I knocked over a lamp. As it crashed to the floor, I left the receiver dangling, a disembodied voice calling out "Ma'am, are you there? Are you okay?"

Almost done. The next part was the worst. I gathered the courage to make some cuts on my arm with a kitchen knife, then allowed the blood to fall on the floor and drip over some of the shards of the lamp. I rinsed off the knife and put it in the dishwasher, then walked through the living room letting blood drip on the carpet and various pieces of furniture I'd knocked over. It definitely looked like something awful happened.

I smiled to myself with self-satisfaction. When Mark got back from Mexico City he was in for a big surprise.

His routine rarely varied. Even with the trip to Mexico this afternoon, I was certain he would take his leisurely drive through Malibu Canyon over to the Valley and then back through Topanga Canyon before going to his office in Century City. He never stopped for coffee or gas during these drives. There would be no way to prove what time he left the house or where he was before he got to the office. Perfect. He would be out of the country before anyone discovered the tableau I set up, so he wouldn't know what happened until he returned.

When I first moved in, I teased him about driving through the canyons and he snapped at me that it cleared his head. Now, the drive was what would do him in. I was ready.

I pictured everything, just like a slide show. When Brittany picked up my message in the evening she would become alarmed. When she tried to return my call there wouldn't be an answer. Knowing Brittany, she'd hop in her car and drive over here. When she arrived she'd find my car in the garage, total disarray inside, blood all over the living room and the doors to the beach open. If I know her, and I do, she'd assume the worst. Her next call would be to 911. It's nice to really know people's patterns.

Then, unless the post office screwed up, the next morning, while the police are here investigating the crime scene, she'll receive my letter, shaky script and all.

Brit,

In case anything happens to me, take this letter to the police. Mark tricked me and turned me into a smuggler. I made quite a few trips for him before I figured out what was going on. The awful truth is I found out I was smuggling millions of dollars of diamonds, emeralds and lord knows what else. Millions! How stupid am I?

I told him I won't do it anymore and he said if I try to leave he will kill me. I'm so scared. It gets worse. He has tapes showing me accepting the packages in London and Amsterdam and discussing how to go through customs with them. He keeps them in his safe. The bastard set it all up to make me look guilty. I'm screwed.

I have to go somewhere he can't find me. I'm leaving tomorrow morning. I sent a letter to the Malibu Sheriff's station too with complete details of everything I know. I managed to find some stuff that blows his story about me being the smuggler out of the water. I've loved having you as a friend.

I'll contact you when I can.

-Mandy

With the stage set, I opened the French doors at the back of the house, and looked out at the water, at the screeching gulls flying overhead and listened to the soft whoosh of the water coming in and going out. There was no other choice. I turned, took a last look around the beautiful rooms, my home for the past year, and shuddered. As I walked out on the sand toward the water, leaving the doors wide open I left this life behind.

Oh, I was careful to cover all the bases. I set up even the smallest details. My murder will be an open and shut case. He will pay.

As Brittany told the homicide detective about the desperate phone call, she sobbed uncontrollably. "Why wasn't I there for her?" She told the story to the detective for the third time. "When I couldn't reach Mandy by phone, I drove here and," her hand swept the room, "found this."

One of the officers got her a glass of water and made her sit down in the next room.

The following day, she called the detective in charge, as she held Mandy's letter in trembling hands. He asked her to come in and talk to him. Now she sat across the desk from him. He nodded and patted his own letter, fanning out the contents of the envelope. He assured her, "We'll get the bastard."

Mark pulled into the driveway, astounded to see yellow crime scene tape. One of the sheriff's deputies extended a warrant, read him his rights and arrested him on the spot, explaining that his house was the scene of a violent murder and significant circumstantial evidence pointed its bony finger at him.

Mark sat slumped in a chair in the stark room as his lawyer railed at him. "She sent them a god-damned letter. Know what else was in the envelope? All kinds of evidence against you."

The lawyer shuffled through his notes, shook his head and said, "They still haven't found her body, but here's what they pieced together. They figure there was a struggle and you accidentally knocked Mandy out or killed her. Then you either carried her into the ocean and dumped her body far out in the water or put it in your car and dumped her somewhere else. You drove to your office, cool as a cucumber, knowing it would look like a break-in that turned into murder. Later in the day you flew to Mexico City as planned, figuring you were home free."

"No-no, I didn't..."

"Yeah. Right! Why did you threaten her, you dumb schmuck? How could you think that would work? Somehow she made a 911 call around nine-twenty in the morning and your struggle is on their tape. You're screwed, pal."

Mark shook his head and rubbed his pounding temples. "No. That's just plain wrong. She was upset, but other than that everything was fine when I left."

"Look asshole, the letter she sent the sheriff includes information about some high stakes smuggling and how you forced her to carry it out. She claimed you threatened to kill her. Told her friend Brittany the same thing. She must have gone through your office from top to bottom. Apparently she found and copied documents that proved how you masterminded the smuggling. Do you have any idea of how incriminating that is? They say she listed flights, dates, descriptions--everything.

He rambled on. "By itself, her letter could be debunked. But documents? What the hell did you have that she could have copied? Didn't we agree there would be nothing about our little business in writing? I know you love to have paper trails, but damn it, man, how could you be so careless?" The color drained from Mark's face leaving two angry red splotches on his cheeks.

"That's ridiculous. There was nothing for her to find."

"Think what you will, but whatever they have, it sounds like a slam dunk. They found some tapes in your safe, too. This is no joke. You're charged with murder. If I'm to help you, I need to know what you did with her. One thing I do know for certain. Mandy's death was not an accident and it was no break-in! Just pray they don't find her body. It will be a lot easier to defend you that way. Level with me, my friend, or you are going to fry and I don't intend to go down with you."

"But..." Mark's hand fumbled in his pocket, then a cunning smile spread over his face. "Oh man. What luck. You're gonna love this." He extended a paper in his hand, waving it back and forth. "I've been fooling around with someone on the side for the past several months. I put her up in a high rise on Wilshire about six months ago. I was with her when I was supposedly killing Mandy."

The attorney said, "Knock it off. Surely you can do better than that. Don't expect me to believe you were with some babe. What are you going to do? Pay some bimbo to say that? Trust me, it won't fly as a defense."

Mark chuckled. "It's on the level."

"And, that scrap of paper you're waving will clear you because..."

"Because, my friend this little piece of paper is my *Get Out Of Jail Free Card*. My alibi. I think the bitch set something up to frame me. She's clever, that one. You know how I love to drive through the canyons before I go to work?"

The lawyer nodded.

"Quiet time. It clears my head. She knew I couldn't account for my time until I got to the office about eleven. Well, here's the thing she didn't know. I haven't done the morning drive since I met Samantha. I crawl into Sam's bed instead and still get to the office around the same time." He winked, clearly feeling better, "I wind up with the same result, a clear head, but it's a lot more fun."

A slight smile started at the corners of the attorney's mouth.

"Anyway I met Sam for breakfast early that morning before we went back to her place." He handed his attorney the charge receipt. "The waitress's name was Jane. I was teasing her and Sam got mad. Jane will remember me. They always remember the big tippers. Look at the time on the charge slip." He poked the slip with his index finger. "Nine-thirty. You said Mandy made the 911 call at nine-twenty. I signed the charge slip in a restaurant in Beverly Hills ten minutes after Mandy made the call." He waved the slip. "Can't be in two places at the same time."

His attorney's smile turned to a wide grin.

"Not only that, but when we went back to Sam's place, we had to get the doorman to let us in because she forgot her key. That was about quarter to ten. So, there is absolutely no way I could have been killing Mandy."

"You are a lucky bastard, you know that?. Good thing you didn't pay cash. Still, they could easily say that maybe you hired someone. So you're not off the hook yet, you understand."

Mark broke in, "Without the frills, what does that mean?"

The attorney scratched his head, thought for a moment, then said, "Well, with the receipt and statements from the waitress, the doorman and your Samantha, we'll get you out on bail. Don't worry about that. I can handle it. Without her body, unless you did hire someone and they can prove it, as I see it, the worst case scenario will have me defending a smuggler, not a killer. Oh yeah, by the way, if they nail you on our little business, don't think about implicating me or you're a dead man."

EPILOGUE

Ten days later the Los Angeles Times carried a story above the fold. What was left of a battered body washed up on the shore about two miles from Hollywood power player Mark Barton's Malibu house. The gruesome remains scared the devil out of a couple strolling at water's edge. They immediately called the sheriff.

A disgusting detailed description followed. Fish had nipped at the corpse destroying most of the face, the skull was fractured, jaw missing, multiple broken bones and missing body parts. The only thing the bones indicated was that the victim had been a female. The water was warm, so deterioration was extensive. Maybe she had been beaten and thrown into the water or maybe it was a drowning accident and the body was mutilated as the result of being bashed against rocks. At any rate, what was left was beyond DNA identification and there wasn't enough of the upper jaw for dental match.

Because the body washed up so close to Mark Barton's luxurious Malibu Beach home, the reporter seized the chance to insinuate that it could be Mandy Blake's remains. However, the story closed with the following statement: Without positive identification the question remains. *What happened to Mandy Blake?*

I lounged on the balcony of my hotel suite at the Empress Hotel in Victoria, Canada, sipping a wonderful glass of chardonnay. When I'd found a hidden stash of bearer bonds along with the documents the day I searched his office, I couldn't believe my good fortune. I only took some and left the rest for him. I'm not greedy. Even if he manages to avoid being convicted for murdering me, there is no way he will ever file a report for the theft of well over a million dollars in bearer bonds, because he can't account for the source of the funds. Remember when I said I had a plan. Anyone can cash bonds like that. I know because I looked it up on the net before I did anything. Like he always said, I'm very clever and analytical.

I raised my glass and offered a toast. "Here's to you Mark and my new identity." Disappearing is child's play when you have plenty of money to do it."

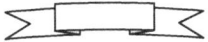

OTHER BOOKS BY MORGAN ST. JAMES

Silver Sisters Mysteries co-authored with Phyllice Bradner

- A Corpse in the Soup
- Seven Deadly Samovars
- Vanishing Act in Vegas

Writers' Tricks of the Trade

- Writers' Tricks of the Trade: 39 Things You Need to Know About the ABCs of Writing Fiction

Stories in these anthologies

- Chicken Soup for the Shopper's Soul
- Chicken Soup for the Soul: Celebrating People Who Make a Difference
- The Mystery of the Green Mist
- Dreamspell Nightmares
- Dreamspell Revenge
- The World Outside the Window
- Writer's Bloc II

Coming in Mid-2012

- Confessions of a Cougar

Writing as Arliss Adams

- Devil's Dance
- The Devil's Due

■

PLEASE VISIT MORGAN'S WEBSITES

For appearance information, workshops, new books and anthologies, links to blogs and more

.

Morgan is available to speak to book clubs anywhere in the world via Skype or in person in the Los Angeles and Las Vegas area.

APPEARANCE SCHEDULE AT:

www.morganstjames-author.com

MORE ABOUT THE SILVER SISTERS MYSTERIES AT

www.silversistersmysteries.com

INCLUDING A CHARACTER INTERVIEW WITH FLOSSIE

❧

READ THE WRITERS' TRICKS OF THE TRADE BLOG AND

MONTHLY

WRITERS' TRICKS OF THE TRADE E-ZINE

http://writerstricksofthetrade.blogspot.com

MORGAN ST. JAMES

Award-winning Author/columnist Morgan St. James co-authors the Silver Sisters Mysteries series, her short stories appear in Chicken Soup for the Soul books and other anthologies.

She writes weekly "Spotlight" and "Writers Tricks of the Trade" columns for the Los Angeles and Las Vegas editions of www.examiner.com, publishes and edits "Writers' Tricks of the Trade E-Zine, and recently released the book "Writers' Tricks of the Trade: 39 Things You Need to Know About the ABCs of Writing Fiction."

Prior to pursuing a writing career, she spent many years as an interior designer specializing in model homes, owned a marketing and promotional company and was in the travel industry. She has traveled extensively nationally and internationally and all of her life experiences enrich her novels and stories. Morgan is an entertaining speaker, presents workshops and frequently appears on author's panels. Morgan splits time between Los Angeles and Las Vegas.

www.morganstjames-author.com

www.silversistersmysteries.com

<u>PREVIEW</u>

COMING IN LATE 2012 - CONFESSIONS OF A COUGAR

One

The pilot's deep voice filled the cabin. "We are approaching Heathrow Airport. Please prepare for landing."

Forty-two years old and finally seeing Europe.

After spending eleven hours shoehorned into a coach seat on the flight from Los Angeles to London, I hoped my aching body wasn't a prelude to what growing old would be like. Even though I'd twisted and turned in every direction possible, it hadn't helped much. Still, I figured there must be a God in heaven because I'd finally fallen asleep somewhere over the Atlantic.

Except for short trips to Mexico and Canada, I'd never been out of the country. My friend Susan had been to Europe before and suggested I wear a comfortable sweat suit on the plane. She was so right. It was sort of like traveling in PJ's.

Years ago the word "cougar" meant a predator capable of stalking and ambushing its prey—a puma or mountain lion. Now don't get me wrong. What I'm talking about here is the other definition—an older woman with a young man. Did I plan it? Never! Let's just say I prefer to think of my adventure as a trip to Europe where my best friend and I happened to have totally unexpected experiences—hot, steamy experiences—but I'm getting ahead of myself.

In a spurt of generosity, my boyfriend Bob had actually treated us to the whole trip. By the way, although he *was* six years younger than me, that slight age difference wasn't what qualified me as a cougar. But, what happened in England did.

The wheels hit the runway with a sound thump and startled me out of a crazy dream. I smoothed my crumpled black velour sweats in an effort to look like I was going to the gym. That's not easy after sleeping several hours twisted into the shape of a pretzel. My legs were stiff and my back ached.

Sue still slept next to me, so I nudged her gently. She blinked, balled her fists and rubbed her eyes. Still in a haze, she murmured softly, "Hal?"

I swallowed hard. Her husband had passed away six months earlier after fighting a long, battle against cancer.

"No, sweetie. It's me, Audrey. Remember, um, Hal is…"

Tears teetered on her bottom lids threatening to overflow. She blinked furiously, then said as though still asleep, "I keep thinking he's still here. You know, alive—." When she looked back at me, her eyes had glazed over. I was one of the few friends she allowed to see what a hard time she was having. On her good days she seemed like her old self, but at other times tears trickled down her face leaving damp trails in their wake. A stoic woman, she struggled to hold them back with steadfast determination.

We gathered our things from the overhead bin then shuffled toward the exit with the rest of the passengers. We were about to embark on an English holiday and it was pure luck. If April and May weren't the busy season in my boyfriend Bob's business, we'd probably still be in L.A.

As we entered Heathrow's terminal a smile lit Sue's face. "Come on, Aud. I think I'm ready to live again."

My heart did a crazy dance. I was really in Jolly Olde England.

During the three years Bob and I had been together, we'd been lucky to carve out even a little time together when "the season"

was in full swing. He practically worked twenty-four/seven during those two months. But he also made tons of money, and Bob loved money.

That last weekend in March, we had what had become our annual romantic dinner. A chance to make the most of our time together before the insanity began. He'd pulled into the restaurant parking lot and handed his Jag over to the valet. The young man flashed a grin. Bob was a generous tipper. "Evening Mr. Stanton."

Everyone knew us at that restaurant, and Bob loved the special treatment.

One of his passions was trading for anything and everything. He'd even traded for the Jag. In fact, I suspect he might have traded his own mother if it was a good deal. During the few transactions I'd watched him negotiate, his face glowed with intense excitement every time he gained the advantage.

It didn't take me long to realize he didn't care about the things he acquired—it was all about the challenge.

In one slick barter deal he traded for a house and boat on Coronado's exclusive Silver Strand near San Diego, but only used them once during the first year. Likewise, he had traded for a magnificent house in Palm Springs the year before. We'd actually spent four days there over Christmas. As for most of the other things he got through his wheeling and dealing, either he never even saw them or gave them to his brother. What a waste. Still, I didn't have the courage to say, "Let me use the Coronado house this weekend," or "I sure would love to drive that car." At one time he actually had five exotic cars just sitting in his driveway while he drove a Toyota Celica.

One, a gorgeous classic Morgan, remained in his driveway covered by a tarp for several months. I saw that car the day he traded for it, and fell in love with it. He hadn't uncovered it since. I kept thinking about the beautiful machine and one day, in a burst of courage, asked him to uncover it. I had to see how cool it was again. He lifted the tarp and we froze in shock. Squirrels had wriggled under it and eaten much of the beautiful wood dash and upholstery. I loved that car. *Why hadn't I asked if I could drive it?*

Anyway, we settled into our favorite booth in the quaint restaurant. Our regular waiter rushed over, flashed a broad smile and presented us with two glasses of excellent Opus One Chardonnay, compliments of the house. Bob always gave him a generous tip and that fellow knew our tastes well. In fact, he knew us so well we never ordered from the menu. That night we just let him bring whatever he thought was best.

Several minutes later he returned with two plates of artfully arranged Alaskan salmon topped with sprigs of dill. The slivers of coral colored fish formed a little mountain atop a bed of wild rice. I recognized a slight teriyaki aroma when the waiter set mine in front of me.

The thing I remember most about that night is how unusually quiet Bob seemed. At last he said, 'Susan's really hurting, isn't she?' Not waiting for my answer, he continued. 'Listen up. I've got a wonderful idea— just the thing for both of you. How would you like to go to England, my treat?'

At first I thought I'd misunderstood. Fork poised, I said, "Did you just say what I think you did? That you want to send me to England...*your* treat?"

Bob smiled and took a bite of the salmon. Pure bliss lit his face. He stopped chewing and said, "That's what I was thinking. You know, I'm going to be absolutely swamped for the next two months and we won't see much of each other. Remember the lease on the cottage in Surrey I traded for a few months ago?"

I nodded. How could I forget when he'd pulled that one off? He had traded a beauty shop and spa in Orange County for a three year lease on the cottage and a small club in London.

"Good. Anyway, it's just sitting there. At first I thought my brother could go check it out and stay for a few weeks. You know how much he loves to prowl the English antique markets. But who am I kidding? He's my partner, so he'll be just as busy as I am. You have vacation time coming. Surprise Susan tomorrow and see if she wants to go."

My mind raced. I knew Susan had been left comfortable enough, so she didn't have to worry about money, but would she want to pay for a European trip? I didn't have to wonder long. Bob's voice broke through my pondering. "By the way, when you ask her if she'd like to go with you, tell her I'll pop for her ticket and some of the expenses. It really will do her good to get away, I'll give you an extra couple of thousand for spending money and you can check the place out for me. What do you think?"

What did I think? That I would forcefully drag my friend Sue to the airport if she had any objections! How great was this? I almost didn't hear what he said next.

"The guy I traded with said there's a Volvo in the garage, so you'll even have a car. Of course, you'll have to get used to driving on the wrong side of the car on the wrong side of the road, but what the heck."

This was almost too much for me to take in at one time. Even with all of his money, Bob and I had taken so few trips and now he was offering to send me to England for three weeks, all expenses paid.

Like everything he negotiated, Bob automatically assumed this was a done deal. He said, "Apparently a nice old couple lives next door and they'll help you girls get settled. It is in the country, so if you don't want to stay there the whole time, you can use the cottage as a base. You know, leave most of your luggage there, take what you need for a day trip, or even a few days and drive around in the Volvo."

The waiter refilled our glasses while I pictured myself in the English countryside. On one hand I was resisting, but in my mind I was already there. I said, "If I'm going to travel all the way to England, I should see London, don't you think?"

Dear, sweet Bob smiled that killer smile of his, the one that made his whole face glow with delight. "Don't even worry your pretty little head about things like that. Once you're there, travel around wherever you want. I'll cover all your expenses, Babe. In fact, if I haven't given you enough and you wind up spending any of your own money, I'll reimburse you. The only thing I'd expect Susan to pay for is her food and any personal things she wants. After all, she'd have to pay for those wherever she is."

He placed his hand over mine and gave it a little squeeze. "I take it if I were you. This is a dream deal, Babe. Come on, say 'yes'. "

www.ingramcontent.com/pod-product-compliance
Lightning Source LLC
Chambersburg PA
CBHW070752120626

46557CB00002B/557